RUCKER
PARK
SeTUP

RUCKER PARK SeTup

PAUL VOLPONI

Viking

Viking

Published by Penguin Group

Penguin Group (USA) Inc., 345 Hudson Street, New York, New York 10014, U.S.A.

Penguin Group (Canada), 90 Eglinton Avenue East, Suite 700, Toronto, Ontario, Canada M4P 2Y3
(a division of Pearson Penguin Canada Inc.)

Penguin Books Ltd, 80 Strand, London WC2R 0RL, England

Penguin Ireland, 25 St Stephen's Green, Dublin 2, Ireland (a division of Penguin Books Ltd)

Penguin Group (Australia), 250 Camberwell Road, Camberwell, Victoria 3124, Australia
(a division of Pearson Australia Group Pty Ltd)

Penguin Books India Pvt Ltd, 11 Community Centre, Panchsheel Park, New Delhi – 110 017, India

Penguin Group (NZ), 67 Apollo Drive, Mairangi Bay, Auckland 1311,
New Zealand (a division of Pearson New Zealand Ltd)

Penguin Books (South Africa) (Pty) Ltd, 24 Sturdee Avenue, Rosebank,
Johannesburg 2196, South Africa

Penguin Books Ltd, Registered Offices: 80 Strand, London WC2R 0RL, England

First published in 2007 by Viking, a member of Penguin Group (USA) Inc.

1 3 5 7 9 10 8 6 4 2

LIBRARY OF CONGRESS CATALOGING-IN-PUBLICATION DATA

Volponi, Paul.

Rucker Park setup / by Paul Volponi.

p. cm.

Summary: While playing in a crucial basketball game on the very court where his best
friend was murdered, Mackey tries to come to terms with his own part in that murder and
decide whether to maintain his silence or tell J.R.'s father and the police what really happened.

ISBN-13: 978-0-670-06130-3 (hardcover)

[1. Basketball—Fiction. 2. Conduct of life—Fiction. 3. Best friends—Fiction. 4. Friendship—Fiction.
5. Murder—Fiction. 6. African Americans—Fiction. 7. Harlem (New York, N.Y.)—Fiction.] I. Title.

PZ7.V8877Ruc 2007

[Fic]—dc22

2006028463

Printed in U.S.A.   Set in Chaparral   Book design by Nancy Brennan

THIS TEXT IS DEDICATED *to every park player who ever threw down like the NBA championship was on the line. Warriors with whom I traded words and elbows, then five minutes later, when the sides changed, had my back with the same fire.*

SPECIAL THANKS: *Joy Peskin, Regina Hayes, Rosemary Stimola, April Volponi, and Jim Cocoros.*

EXTRA SPECIAL THANKS: *Tommy "Pirate" Zittel, a park basketball legend in Brooklyn and Queens for half a century.*

RUCKER PARK SeTuP

Prologue

A FATHER SHOULDN'T have to outlive his own son. It's not right.

My pops died when I was too little to remember. And without the pictures my mom kept, I wouldn't even know what he looked like.

Stove was like my second pops, and he did things with me I never got a chance to do with my real flesh and blood. His son, J.R., was my best friend since fifth grade and lived in the same apartment building as me. It didn't matter that I'm black and they're Puerto Rican. We got to be almost family. But I don't deserve any more best friends. Not after the way I played J.R., and ran off when he needed me the most.

I'd heard the sirens screaming up Frederick Douglass Boulevard, so I figured it was safe to get my chicken-ass back to the park. I watched from across the street and wouldn't get any closer. J.R. was lying on the basketball court under a green sheet, and his blood was on the ground all around him. Everything I'd done was weighing down on me, till moving my feet was like lifting two solid blocks of cement.

People were looking at me because they knew how tight we were. I didn't want to see inside anymore and tried to keep my eyes on the high fence around Rucker Park. Then I saw Stove coming up the block in his mailman's suit, pushing a cart full of letters.

"That's the boy's father," somebody whispered, and the blood pumping inside me turned ice-cold.

I heard a voice beg Stove not to look. I shut my eyes tight but couldn't stop from opening them again.

An old lady came out of the crowd and threw her arms around Stove. He was down on one knee, crying in the street.

My best friend had just got stabbed to death right in front of me, and I didn't lift a finger to help him. I was too scared, and I knew that I still had to worry about my own skin.

I saw my reflection in a car window and wanted to spit on it.

I remembered Stove telling J.R. about the day he

was born. How he put his hand on J.R.'s chest to feel his heart beating. Only now my ears were stuck on the sound of kids bouncing basketballs. They were pounding the sidewalk, over and over, like heartbeats gone wild.

J.R. AND ME grew up the same—dreaming about winning the big basketball tournament at Rucker Park. We wanted it so bad that it got to be in our blood. We played on that court all the time, except those nights in August, when we'd just watch with our mouths hanging open. That's when the best pickup teams in the city would throw down in the middle of Harlem, right around the block from where we lived.

We could see it perfect from J.R.'s window. But we always wanted to be inside the park so we could feel it, too. Rucker Park is where some of the greatest pro ballers ever, like Dr. J and Wilt Chamberlain, squared off against street legends—guys with tags like Goat and Helicopter. Stove reffed lots of those famous games, before either J.R. or me was born. He's the head ref at the tournament now and always works the championship game.

J.R.'s pops had reffed our games since we were eleven years old, playing youth league. He never cut us a single break. Any call that was close went against us. I guess Stove wanted to teach J.R. and me to stand on our own, and show people he blew an honest whistle.

J.R. used to complain to his mother about it all the time, before she died from cancer a few years back.

"I thought blood was supposed to be thicker than water," he'd say to her, knowing his pops was listening in.

Then Stove would rip back, "There's only sweat on a basketball court, Mami. And it's salty, just like a baby's tears."

I was at J.R.'s crib the night Stove called from the hospital to say she'd passed away. We looked at pictures from her last birthday party, and J.R. couldn't stop crying. I left when Stove got home. But the second I walked out the door, I broke down, too. I sat on the stairs between floors in our building, bawling my eyes out.

That's when J.R. and his pops started to get even closer. And maybe I was a little jealous, because I couldn't stand even being in the same house with my mom's new husband and his big mouth.

The tournament here last summer was our first as players. We were going into our junior year then and were already starters on the squad at George Washington High School. But we mostly rode the bench behind older dudes with bigger bodies on a tournament team at Rucker Park.

Since then, J.R. shot up two more inches, to six-three. I was almost as tall, and we both hit the weights hard. We took George Washington deep into the play-offs this year, losing the semifinal game at Madison Square Garden. We were starstruck just to be standing on that court, looking up at all those seats. And we left the locker room there feeling like pros already.

J.R. got named All-City in the *Daily News*, and I got Honorable Mention. That's when the colleges started sending us letters and our phones started ringing off the hook. Stove sat us down with an SAT prep book every night, and that gave me a good excuse to keep out of my house.

But Stove watched out for who came around, too.

"Street agents are fishin' for a piece of every kid with a future on the court. Snakes with cars and money will want to be your best friend. They front for management companies that can't contact a kid till he's done playin' in college and ready to turn pro," Stove warned us all the time. "They get their hooks into as many kids as they can. It's like buying up a hundred lottery tickets, and hopin' one hits big. I've seen them turn a poor kid's head with a new pair of sneakers."

That's why J.R.'s pops wouldn't let us play for Fat Anthony. He coaches Non-Fiction—a street team that's won the Rucker Park Tournament four times. Stove grew up with Anthony and knows his bag of tricks inside out. Everybody at the park knows Fat Anthony delivers kids to certain agents. That he bets on the games, and sometimes his players get a taste of that money.

"If college coaches hear you're mixed up in gambling, they'll give that scholarship to somebody else," said Stove. "It's not a game to Anthony. And son, I don't want you or Mackey mixed up in any of his dirty business."

I'd heard a new team called the Greenbacks was going after the best high-school talent around. J-Greene, a big-time rapper, started it up for the publicity and named the squad after his new CD, *In It for the Greenbacks*.

Greene showed up at Rucker Park with a fly shorty on each arm, and Tommy Mitchell, who used to play pro ball for the New York Knicks. Mitchell was coaching the Greenbacks. He already knew about J.R. and me, and wanted us both on the squad.

I didn't even have to think about it, but J.R. did.

"I definitely want to be down," J.R. told them. "But I gotta run it by my pops first."

Greene shot us a look like we were little kids. Then he turned to Mitchell and said, "I thought we was recruitin' men to wear my name."

"Trust me on this, G," said Mitchell, "these two got man-style game."

"Bless them!" barked Greene, snapping his fingers.

That's when his shorties gave us each a jersey the color of money, and a long kiss on the cheek.

"I get what I want," said Greene. "And when the honeys see you in those, and we win Rucker Park, you'll be gettin' plenty, too."

J.R. spent that whole night trying to convince his pops to let him join. I played him one of Greene's raps, but Stove hated it. He said it made Harlem sound like a war zone. After that, we kept hitting on how much we could learn from Tommy Mitchell, till J.R.'s pops finally caved and said it was all right.

We had a squad full of high-school all-stars, and a couple of ex-college players with muscle to back us up. And after our first practice together, J.R. and me knew the Greenbacks were going to be the bomb.

In our first tournament game, we were winning by almost forty points. The other team had a crew of older cats who couldn't keep up. But then we started rubbing it in, acting like real hot dogs. Mitchell got pissed over that and benched some of our guys.

Stove reffed that one and didn't stop the clock once inside the last five minutes. He was trying to get that spanking over with fast, before that other team figured they had to fight us to keep from looking like assholes.

Acorn announces the games at Rucker Park. He owns the barbershop down the block, and everybody knows him. He's big and thick, with a voice like Barry White from my mom's old records.

During the games, Acorn sits by the side of the court with a microphone in his hand. He's always got something quick to say. If you make a bonehead play, Acorn will dis you good in front of everybody. But when you do something right, he'll give you props for it, too.

If you're really special, Acorn gives you a nickname. And if the crowd hoots and hollers enough at that tag, it'll stick. It was Acorn who blessed some of the greatest street ballers with the tags that everybody knows them by.

The last few minutes of that first game was like a personal highlight tape of my best plays ever. It started with a pass I made through some dude's legs right to J.R. for an easy basket. The next time down court, I fired the ball off the backboard, and it looked like I was passing it to myself. Three guys from the other team came charging at me. But instead of catching the ball, I slapped it to J.R. for an open layup, and everybody watching roared.

"Hold the mustard on that hot dog!" Acorn echoed through Rucker Park.

Every time I touched the ball after that, Acorn called me "Hold the Mustard."

The crowd was loving it, too, till Mitchell yanked me from the game for showboating. But when I got to the sideline, Greene threw both arms around me, and Mitchell backed off. When the game ended, Greene brought the whole squad with him out to center court and rapped his big hit, "Up Yours."

That night, I went home with J.R. and his pops. There was leftover stew for supper, and a whole loaf of bread we finished off with the brown gravy. The walls held on to every bit of heat from that day, so Stove opened the windows wide, hoping for a breeze.

All J.R. and me could talk about was winning the championship, and how maybe Non-Fiction was the only crew that could keep us from it.

"You want something so bad, for so long. Then it's right in front of you," said J.R. over the TV and noise from the street. "You gotta check yourself to make sure it's really happenin'. And you gotta watch out, so you don't screw up and give it away, especially to that bastard Fat Anthony."

"But it's sweet!" I told him.

"Sweeter for you with that new tag," said J.R., dribbling a pretend ball between his legs, till we both cracked up laughing.

Then J.R. went to his bedroom window to find the star his mother taught him to wish on. She said it was the same star from the Puerto Rican flag and that it would always watch over him. But I didn't believe in that kind of stuff and stayed in the kitchen with Stove.

"You need *confianza*—faith in things, Mackey," said Stove. "Or else you better believe in yourself more than anything."

Those were just words to me then, with nothing behind them. But over the last few weeks they've been roaring in my head.

Now the championship game's in front of *me*. Rucker Park's packed tonight to see the Greenbacks finally take on Non-Fiction. But I'm not sure how much I believe in myself anymore, or what's really inside of me.

Stove's got the game ball under his arm and a whistle hanging from his neck. Only J.R.'s not here—because I fucked up so bad. And his killer's standing right there, cool as anything, like he doesn't have to think twice about me giving him up.

2

WE WERE SUPPOSED to play Non-Fiction the second week of the tournament, but that game got canceled after J.R. was killed.

Greene showed up at the park a few nights before that. He left his Lexus right in front of the hydrant with the engine running and walked onto the court. He had on a Greenbacks jersey and a thick rope chain with a gold dollar sign hanging from it, studded in diamonds. Kids were all over him for his autograph when Fat Anthony started talking trash.

"Old-timers—that's all those Greenies beat. They blew past dudes with kids of their own," cracked Fat Anthony.

"You dis my clan to my face and it's on, Pops," Greene shot back. "I'm not gonna cut you slack 'cause of your years."

J.R. and me thought they were going to throw down right then, and probably so did the hundred other eyes and ears glued to them.

"Talk's cheap around here, son," said Fat Anthony. "What else you got to put up besides your fists?"

Greene pulled a fat roll of bills from his pocket and waved it in Anthony's face. When the spit stopped flying, they had a five-thousand-dollar bet riding on the game. Greene even spotted him five points. And I swear, I saw Fat Anthony fight back a grin.

"It won't even be a game!" snarled Greene. "My team's like assassins. They'll eat up those five points in the first minute. I woulda gave you ten points if you asked for it, sucka. You're ass-stupid. You don't know shit 'bout makin' deals, Doughboy!"

But I guess Fat Anthony already got what he wanted, because after that he pulled a deaf-mute act. He just let Greene run his mouth and wouldn't answer back.

"See, you know you can't trade words with me. That's *my* business," said Greene, grabbing the bling around his neck. "*You* hold your tongue. After the game, *I'll* be holdin' your money!"

That whole scene only ended when Greene chased after the cop who left a ticket on the windshield of his whip.

The day before the game with the Greenbacks, J.R.

and me were shooting baskets at the park. Fat Anthony was talking to us from the sideline, saying how heroes are made in close games.

"People will always remember who made the winning shot in a tight game," said Fat Anthony. "And anything less than that five-point spread's tight enough for me. The crowd wants to see—"

Fat Anthony pulled up short on his words, seeing Stove over his shoulder.

"Here comes the law on the court," laughed Anthony. "I better quit talkin' 'bout the points."

Stove pretended like Fat Anthony wasn't even there and started feeding us passes so we could work on our jumpers. Anthony watched us drain maybe a dozen shots in a row. Then he asked Stove why he wouldn't ever let J.R. and me play for him in the tournament.

"Because my father's always looking out for us," answered J.R., raising up from the top of the circle and burying another one.

"That's all right," laughed Fat Anthony. "I'm even glad your pops is working the game tomorrow. I know he'll keep things right."

Then Fat Anthony stuck out his hand, and after a second, Stove shook it.

"I just hope it's a game people remember for the

action *on* the court," said Stove. "Not for what happens on the *side*."

"And I know if there's a close call, it won't go your son's way. You're just like that," said Fat Anthony, smiling like a guy who had a bet he couldn't lose.

I spent that whole next morning with J.R., before he got killed. We were trying to come up with a tag for him that would go with Hold the Mustard. We went through every kind of food in my refrigerator, looking for something that would fit. It was all laid out on the table next to the mustard. But nothing really clicked. Then my mom came in and yelled at us for making a mess out of her kitchen. But I was just happy to be home without her damn husband there to put me down, or hollering at me to get a part-time job instead of playing ball. J.R. knew it, too, and even made a fuss over my new nickname in front of her.

"As long as you two keep clear of trouble, I don't care what your friends call you," Mom said, calming down enough to hug us both. "Now put everything back in that fridge the way I had it."

In the end, there were a couple of names we thought were all right. So we wrote them out and took the list to Acorn at his barbershop. The place was packed, but he looked up from giving a haircut and smiled when we walked in.

"Maybe one day, I'll have these boys' pictures up with the rest of them," said Acorn for everybody to hear.

The back wall of his shop is covered with pictures of famous ballers who threw down at Rucker Park. There's Doctor, Hawk, Pee Wee, Skates, Big Dipper, and maybe a hundred more. And lots of them got their tags straight from Acorn's mouth.

But when we showed him the list, Acorn's face turned funny. He looked it over for a minute like he was serious. Then he busted out laughing in that big voice.

"You boys want names?" asked Acorn, trying to hold himself together. "How about the Dummy Brothers?"

That's when everybody in the shop started laughing at us, too.

"Listen to what they came up with," crowed Acorn. "'Sweet Relish!' Can you imagine that?"

"You can't just choose yourself a nickname," said the man getting a haircut. "That would be cheatin'."

"It's got to come to Acorn natural-like, durin' a game," another dude kicked in.

Then Acorn grabbed J.R. around the shoulders and stood him in front of the mirror.

"Now you can stand here all day tellin' everybody how good-looking you are," said Acorn. "But you're better off waitin' for it to come from somebody else's mouth first. It's the same with nicknames."

We were almost out the door when an old man said, "It's a good thing those boys got each other to talk to, 'cause nobody else in this world would take 'em serious."

Outside, we could still hear them laughing. Then somebody opened the door to the shop, and it got louder for a few seconds, till the door got closed again.

The rest of our time together, J.R. was pissed at me.

"Pickin' out a tag was mostly your idea," said J.R. "Only Acorn made more fun of me than you."

But nobody's laughing at Rucker Park tonight. It's all business. Even for the warm-ups, kids got their game faces screwed on tight. I can hear the snap in every pass on the layup line. Nobody's going light. It's all power dunks, and everybody's trying to rip the rim right off the damn backboard. Sometimes you can scare another squad right out of the game when you got it cooking in the drills. But you don't scare anybody off when you're playing for the championship at Rucker Park. Not when both teams got confidence and know they belong.

Non-Fiction's real organized, and got everything planned out. They clap hands twice when the guy at the front of their layup line drives for the hoop. The third beat is supposed to be the sound of him throwing it down. And when it's working right, it sounds like drums beating.

We don't have anything worked out together for the warm-ups. Kids on our team go dolo, and do whatever they feel. Every time one of our guys throws down a monster jam, the crowd goes crazy. Then nobody can hear that bullshit clapping from the other side of the court, and that's what we want.

Both teams want to one-up each other for the crowd and really rock the house. Lots of people are still open about which team to pull for, and both squads want to win them over bad. Crowds at Rucker Park are loud, and almost right on top of the court. When they're all together on something, their voice can be like a sledgehammer that no team wants to get hit with.

I can even hear them screaming from outside the fence and down the block. There are kids sitting in trees and on the tops of streetlights. The park's mobbed, and people are still lined up on the sidewalk waiting to get inside. It takes a while because everybody gets patted down by the cops for weapons and bottles, even the players.

Half the windows on J.R.'s side of our building are filled up with people hanging out of them. I can see his bedroom window clear as anything. It's closed up tight, with the shade pulled down.

Most kids on the court can really sky. I can dunk a

ball okay, but I'm not going to turn any heads like that. My game is all about being fast on my feet, so I try to lay the ball in with some real style behind it.

I cradle the pass on my fingertips, like somebody tossed me a baby from the window in a fire. I drive for the basket going a hundred miles an hour. Then I let every muscle in my body go easy. Everybody's eyes are still moving quick to keep up. That's when I find my own space, where everything else just slides by, and nothing can touch me. I plant my left foot and bring the ball over my head. And just as I finger-roll it to the rim, I flip it soft and high. I start back down to the ground the same time as the ball. The net jiggles as it slips through, and I send that same little wave down my shoulders to my hips.

The crowd oohs and aahs like I brushed them with a feather. Then I jog back to the end of the line. Only I keep my eyes up the whole way, so I don't see the spot on the court where J.R. got killed.

Greene grabs the mike out of Acorn's hand and starts rapping about me.

"They call him Hold the Mustard,
But the brother's smooth like custard.
If there's a move he'll bust it . . ."

The whole park's yelling my name, and I start to feel good inside. Then I see J.R.'s pops. I know he's the ref and is supposed to stay even. But that cold look on his face turns me blank, till it robs me of everything.

Stove keeps waiting to hear something different out of my mouth.

"That's everything I saw!" I told him, the same way I practiced over and over to sell the cops on it. "There's nothin' I'm leavin' out! That's how it went down! Why do I gotta keep sayin' it?"

Anyway, nothing's going to bring back J.R.

Mackey told the cops it was two kids he'd never seen before. That they were playing two-man when one of them started arguing with J.R. over a foul call. Then the kid went loco and pulled a knife. But it wasn't like J.R. to get heated over a pickup game, or go out looking for a run when he had the tournament that night. No one else saw a thing, and that didn't make sense to me, either. The regulars at the park are always checking out newjacks who come to play on their turf. They'd drop a dime on any stranger who touched somebody from the neighborhood. But Mackey hasn't gone back on a word of his story. And he hasn't been able to look me in the eye since.

I hear that damn bet Anthony and Greene made got carried over to tonight, after the first game got canceled because of J.R. That's something else that doesn't sit right with me.

The cancer that took Carmen was from God, but I know this was even dirtier than Mackey's letting on.

An official basketball weighs twenty-one and one-quarter ounces. I've started enough games by tossing one up at center court to know. But every ball here feels heavier than that to me.

STOVE PLAYED BALL in this park when he was a kid. Back when it was called the 155th Street Playground, and Holcombe Rucker, the guy who thought up the tournament, was still alive. J.R. and me heard Stove's stories about the old days so many times, it was almost like we lived them out ourselves.

"Rucker worked for the Parks Department. He didn't have a dime behind him, so he used scoreboards made from oak tag, tied up to fences. Then the pros started showing up to play. They loved the freedom of street ball, and so did everybody who came out to watch," J.R.'s pops would tell us. "Once before a game, the teams needed a few more balls to shoot around with and get loose. A pro, big enough to block out the sun, said to me, 'Hey, kid, let me hold that ball for a while.' He caught my throw in one hand, and squeezed it like an orange. Then I watched them shoot around with *my* ball, following it from player to player. I took that ball to bed with me for the rest of the summer."

Stove replayed moves for us that went down smooth as silk. Moves invented on the spot that couldn't be drawn up ahead of time with a pencil and paper, and even had to be explained to the guys who made them after the game. Lots of them were made by street ballers—guys who never wore a uniform in their lives, except for maybe going shirts or skins in the street. But they got a chance to go up against pros in front of a crowd at Rucker Park, and played their hearts out.

Most of the pro ballers stopped coming to Rucker when their contracts got so many zeros in them that they couldn't afford to get hurt in a park game. There were only a couple of pros who played this year. But J.R. and me made a pact that even after we hit it big in the NBA, we'd play in the tournament together every summer, no matter what.

"Money will never push us off our love for the game. We're gonna recognize where we come from and not disrespect the park," J.R. said before our first tournament game, making a fist for me to give him a pound.

"The love of ball ahead of everything," I said, connecting my fist to his.

But I shit all over that promise the first time Fat Anthony put a dime in front of me.

And now I can't even tell J.R. how sorry I am.

J.R. always knew what I was thinking on the court. It was like he could see the moves being born in my mind at the same time I did. Only J.R. couldn't see everything inside of me. He didn't know what I got myself into, or how it got him killed. But I got to keep all that strapped down tight. I need to hold up the deal I made—and find a way to win the championship, too.

The horn sounds to end the warm-ups, and both squads go back to their benches. Acorn is out in the middle of the court, talking to the crowd. There are people here from all over the city, and lots of them never heard about J.R.

"Right here on this court, we lost a member of our Rucker Park family to an act of violence a few weeks back. He was more than a promising young player. He was already a superstar son, friend, teammate, and member of this community. Despite a heavy heart, his father is here to ref the game tonight because this championship meant so much to his son," says Acorn, turning his eyes to Stove. "I want you all to join me in a moment of silence for Nicolas Vasquez Jr. Most of you knew him as J.R."

Except for the traffic on Frederick Douglass Boulevard, there isn't a sound.

Stove's standing straight, like a statue, with his head bowed down.

I see lots of people holding back tears. But nothing gets to that murdering fuck. He just stands there with his chin in his chest, like he's talking to God. He's the reason everybody's praying for J.R. And it doesn't bother him one damn bit.

When that silence is over, kids drop their hands on my back and shoulders, like I deserve some kind of sympathy. Only I don't.

Mitchell huddles us up and goes through the first few plays he wants to run. Then we all put our hands on top of each other's in a big pile, and Mitchell gives us a speech about playing hard.

"This is what you've all been dreamin' about," says Mitchell. "Now you each gotta look inside yourself and see what's really there. And don't forget—when you let yourself down, you fail your brother, too."

My eyes are already down on the ground.

Everybody's got J.R.'s initials on their sneakers to remember him.

His good kicks are still in the hallway at my crib, and I won't touch them for anything.

J.R.'s mom once taught mine how to make Spanish rice and beans. We were going to eat that at my place and change there before the game, while my mother's husband was still at work.

Sometimes I see J.R. standing inside those sneakers. He just looks at me with his arms folded on top of his chest. I keep thinking how he must know everything from where he is. But his face is all calm, and he's not mad or anything.

He just looks at me, like he's waiting for me to set things right.

But that's easy for J.R. He's safe now, and nobody can touch him anymore. I still got to walk these streets and be out here playing ball so I can make it one day.

"Let me hear it, everybody! On three!" says Mitchell.

"One, two, three—*teamwork*!" kids shout.

It blasts from my throat, too, but it doesn't have any feeling.

Fat Anthony's jawing at his players in their huddle. I can see his face twist with every word he pushes out of his mouth.

Then they circle up tighter and shout, "Just win!"

Fat Anthony follows them halfway onto the court.

"Remember, if you fuck up out there, don't even

come back to the bench. I only got seats for winners," says Anthony. "Yo mama might still love you, but I won't!"

J.R.'s pops stands at center court, between the two tallest kids. He tosses the ball up higher than both of them can reach, and the crowd lets out a noise that starts something burning inside of me.

There's no more talk, and nothing to think about. There's just basketball.

A kid in green rips the rock away from a white jersey, and we head up court with the ball. Mitchell called my number for the first play. Two of our kids step out in front of me, and I move around a double-screen. The guy that's guarding me gets caught up in all the traffic. I sprint alone past the spot where J.R. got killed. I let an open shot fly from the corner, and the ball's through the net before my feet touch the ground again.

"Ladies and gentlemen, you better Hold the Mustard tonight," echoes Acorn. "It's two to nothing, Green-backs."

I look up, and Stove is running back down court, right next to me. But before our eyes come together, I turn away to find my man on defense.

Both teams score a basket on their next possession. Then the ball kicks out-of-bounds off two kids fighting for it. Hamilton, the other ref on the court, isn't sure who touched it last, and looks at Stove for help. Finally Hamilton points our way. That's when Fat Anthony flips, and starts screaming at Hamilton like it's the biggest play of the game.

"You don't make a call against my team unless *you* see it!" fires Anthony. "Folks didn't fill this park to hear you blow that tin whistle!"

Hamilton walks off from Fat Anthony, and the crowd lets him hear it.

"*Zebra— Zebra! We don't need ya—We don't need ya!*"

This is Hamilton's first championship game at Rucker Park, and Fat Anthony's working him hard. He's trying to get into Hamilton's head, so a big call at the end of the game might go his way.

Fat Anthony's got two goons on his squad, and getting close to the basket's like being in a football game. It's that rough.

The painted rectangle from the backboard to the foul line, fifteen feet away, is called "The House." Only there aren't any welcome mats for kids in different colored jerseys, just elbows and forearms to greet you.

That crap stops lots of teams without any heart. But nobody on our side's backing down an inch, especially in front of a crowd like this.

Non-Fiction misses a shot, and I push the ball back

the other way in a hurry. Two of Fat Anthony's guys follow after me, so I know somebody's running free. I look
up on instinct, expecting to see J.R. waving his arms,
like I couldn't get him the ball fast enough.

But J.R.'s not here.

There's a kid in green alone on the other side of the
court. I whip him a pass, and he drives for the hoop.
That's when one of Anthony's goons hammers him hard
to the ground.

Three Non-Fiction dudes are standing over him.

"Not in our house!" one of them pops off.

Hamilton is already between them, and everybody
in green is rushing over to stick up for their man. Players on both benches are standing, and Mitchell's holding
back our guys.

Greene jumps the scorer's table and makes a run
at Fat Anthony, till two cops get in front of him. But
Anthony doesn't budge. He just stares straight at
Greene, and the corners of his mouth curl up in a smile.
The crowd is split between boos and cheers. And Stove
is in the middle of everything, laying down the law.

Stove gets Mitchell and Fat Anthony out at center
court, away from everybody. But Stove is so hyped that
half the park can hear his speech.

"I'll kick the next player out of this game who crosses

the line. I don't care how important he is to your team," warns Stove. "I don't referee football or boxing, just hoops!"

Then everything settles down, and the game starts up again.

Players on both squads are flat-out fast. Only Stove hasn't been on a court in a few weeks. There are circles under his eyes, and he's breathing hard to keep up. And the next time the ball goes out-of-bounds, Stove stalls for time by walking it over to the scorer's table and wiping it dry. But it's mostly slick from his own sweat.

I step in front of a pass headed for a Non-Fiction kid and jet the other way with it. They've got two guys back between me and the basket, so I rocket straight for the first one. A couple of steps before him, I dip my head and shoulders to the right. Soon as he bites, I cross over to my left. The guy almost breaks his ankles trying to stay with me and falls to the floor with his feet twisted in a knot.

"He got corkscrewed!" screams Acorn.

There's a goon planted under the hoop, waiting for me. I cup the ball in my right hand and show it to that bonehead. Then I bring it behind my back, like I'm going to switch hands. I hesitate, and when the rock doesn't come out on the left side, he gambles on the right. But I switched hands all along, and I go sailing past.

He scrapes my shoulder, and I scoop the ball into the basket, high off the backboard. Stove's and Hamilton's cheeks puff up to blow their whistles, and they both bring one arm down through the air. It's a foul. That basket counts, and I got a chance for a three-point play.

Only I never heard those whistles. Right then, you couldn't hear a car horn blowing on the court. Everyone at Rucker Park was going wild, celebrating that move I made.

"I don't care if it's yellow, spicy brown, or even *di*-jon. Hold the Mustard 'cause that was a foot-long hot dog delivered bone dry," bellows Acorn.

Before I step to the foul line, Fat Anthony calls a time-out to quiet the crowd. Then he shoots me a look, like I better start doing what I'm supposed to, quick.

4

DON'T SMILE! JUST don't smile! I got to walk off this court with a straight face. People need to think this is nothing for me. That I make those kinds of plays every day. Kids can give me high fives all they want, my face isn't going to move a muscle.

Greene and his posse are standing on chairs, cheering. And every time they throw their arms up, the crowd screams, "Hold the Mustard!" till even the trees start to shake with my name.

That's how it was when Nike shot their TV commercial here with Vinsanity, the most vicious dunker in the NBA. He played in the Olympics, too, and even jumped over some foreign dude from head to toe on a dunk.

Vinsanity came to Rucker to play in a tournament game a few years back, and everybody was stoked to see him. Only the sky opened up and it poured buckets, so the game got moved inside, to a junior-high gym.

The place was mobbed, but J.R. and me fought our way into the first row. People came in soaked to the skin and were dripping puddles on the floor. The windows were stuck closed and the whole gym smelled like wet dog, but nobody minded.

"I just wanna see Vinsanity lay down some insane move," said J.R.

A couple of minutes into the game, Vinsanity picked off a pass and streaked to the hoop alone. Stove back-pedaled his ass off to keep close to him and probably had the best view of anybody.

"*¡Dios mío!* This is it!" said J.R., like it was his birth-day and Christmas rolled into one.

Vinsanity climbed some invisible ladder and didn't stop till his knees were as high as Stove's head. Then he brought the rock back down for everybody to see, before he pounded the rim with it.

I swear, the roof jumped five feet off of that gym from all the noise.

"It's like going to church, and seeing God," I said, after I got down off my toes.

Lots of people must have felt that way, because Nike made a commercial about *that* slam. Only they shot it at Rucker Park, and not the gym.

They dressed everybody up "old school," like back in

the days when lots of the pros took their summer vacations at Rucker. Vinsanity had on a throwback jersey and a big Afro wig. Stove played the ref on the court, and J.R. and me even got twenty-five bucks apiece to be part of the crowd.

Vinsanity copied the same move he made in the gym, and everybody went wild for the cameras. They made him do it maybe ten times, and we screamed on every one.

"No matter what they do, nothin' can match the way it felt that night," I told J.R. while they were filming. "'Cause after somethin' like that, everything else is just pretend."

But the championship game, and everything else I'm feeling here tonight, is *too* real.

This is *my* time. I got to be the man out here right now. Before it's over, I might have to play bad for a while to keep this game close. I'm not even sure I know how, without everybody in Rucker Park figuring it out. But I can change my mind, too. I can keep on scoring, till we win by fifty points. The crowd will be all over me after the game, and Fat Anthony won't be able to get close. Then I'd just lay low for the next year and take a college scholarship out of state. I'd cut Anthony a fat check from my first pro contract, and we'd be square. . . .

Screw that shit!

Non-Fiction just needs to pump their game up, so I can stay on top of mine.

The rest of our squad jumps up off the bench, so the starters can sit and catch a blow. Mitchell kneels in front of us with a clipboard, and everybody circles around.

"Don't get caught up in how easy this is," says Mitchell. "They're a good team, and they're gonna make adjustments."

Mitchell's drawing *X*s and *O*s, and everybody's eyes are glued.

But I hear the crowd and my mind goes to the times J.R. and me pretended there were people lined up outside this fence to see *us* play. We'd make our own crowd noise by cupping our hands over our mouths and screaming loud. Only that was nothing compared to the way it sounds right now.

J.R. would count down the last seconds: "Five . . . four . . . three . . ."

Then he'd pass me the ball, and I'd heave it up from half-court.

While the shot was still in the air, we'd be finishing counting together: "Two . . . one . . . *buzzzz.*"

If the shot was good we'd run around the court and go crazy, like we'd just won the championship. If it missed, we'd start over with J.R. taking the next shot. We could spend an hour going back and forth getting it to come out right. And we wouldn't even think about quitting till it did.

Look at that fuck's face.

He thinks I'm his boy. That I'm going to put money in his pocket and keep my mouth shut about what he did to J.R., too. I hate how much he thinks I'm under his thumb, because I'm not.

I never snitched on anybody in my life. And if I did now, it would be all over the TV and newspapers. Everybody would know how I screwed over my best friend and sold out my team for money. Then I could never show my face at Rucker Park again.

Mitchell jumps to his feet, and everybody's moving. The time-out's over.

J.R.'s pops is waiting under the basket, flipping the ball up at the rim with one hand. It goes straight in, and the crowd gives him a cheer.

Stove got his tag playing in the tournament, too.

"If I got my feet set, I could be on fire shooting the ball. That's how they got to call me 'Stove,'" he'd tell anybody who'd listen.

But J.R. and his mom used to snap on him all the time.

"Now that tag's for your stomach, like a potbellied stove," needled J.R.

"A stove that don't throw off the kind of heat it used to, either," she'd stick on top of it.

Stove twists the ball between his hands. His eyes are sharp like razors, and I can feel them running over every inch of me. He's got a look on his face harder than any player's on the court. And I know he's challenging me with it.

It's a look that says, *Mackey, you're a liar! And I'm not backing off!*

"You're my warrior out there, Mustard!" shouts Greene from behind me. "Be a Greenback all the way!"

But I never turn around, and his words just bounce off my back.

I set myself at the foul line to finish that three-point play, and Stove sends me the ball with some zip. But it's like ice in my hands, and I can't feel the grips.

I drop my head and take a deep breath. Then I raise up, and let the shot go. It doesn't roll off my fingertips like it's supposed to, and comes out of my hand flat.

The shot's way short. But it catches the front lip of the basket, and spins backwards. It rolls around till it sits dead still on the rim, and can't stay balanced there anymore. Then it falls through the hoop to the floor.

"That's a real shooter's roll," announces Acorn. "It's seven to two, Greenbacks."

That's when my eyes lock up with Fat Anthony's. He's grilling me fierce. He's probably not sure if he can trust me. His squad's already down by five points, and it's mostly because of my scoring.

Fat Anthony's always telling stories about the bets he loses. I guess that's because if he told about every time he won, nobody would put their money up against him. He's even got one about the Goat, a playground legend from back in the day, who skinned Fat Anthony for fifty bucks.

"Goat was only six-one, but he could jump out of his goddamn shoes," Anthony told a bunch of us at the park one time. "He was sayin' how he could dunk backwards twenty times straight—no problem. I pushed it up to thirty times and challenged him in front of a crowd so he couldn't back down."

Fat Anthony said how the Goat started out gliding, like he wasn't even jumping. Then once he hit twenty, he started to strain. His legs turned to jelly on the last few dunks, and he just cleared the rim. But he did it. The Goat dunked backwards thirty times in a row, and Fat Anthony had to cough up the cash.

"Like always, I was the bad guy, and everybody was rooting against me. Goat didn't even have the fifty bucks to put up. Two or three dudes helped to stake him, so they were all countin' as my money hit his hand. And all

I had was a pocketful of tens. It felt like forever. 'Ten . . . twenty . . . thirty . . . forty . . . fifty!' everybody shouted. I'd have given anything to have a fifty-dollar-bill on me, just to make it go faster!" said Fat Anthony.

I thought about how it would kill Fat Anthony to pay off Greene—because I know there's no such thing as a five-thousand-dollar-bill.

Stove told J.R. and me how the Goat got hooked on heroin and went to jail instead of the pros. The Goat was gone from around here for a long time. But years later, he got himself together and made it back to the park. It didn't matter that he was old and his skills were used up. Kids had heard so much about his game, they lined up just to see if he was for real. The Goat died a few years back. His heart gave out, maybe from all the abuse. And the one time I got to shake his hand, I could almost feel Fat Anthony's money piling up inside his palm.

A Non-Fiction player tries to sneak a pass by me. I reach out to steal it, without thinking. Then I remember Fat Anthony. So I slap the ball out-of-bounds instead, and Non-Fiction keeps possession.

I turn my head to see Fat Anthony. I thought he'd be happy with what I did. But he's got a look on his face like he'd kill me if he could, right here in front of everybody.

Fat Anthony

I'll stare that boy down for as long as it takes. He needs to understand—whatever he does for me out there isn't good enough. He thinks this is his party, and he's just doing a little job for me on the side. But that's wrong. All wrong! I bought his ass, plain and simple. It took just five hundred dollars to turn his head around. Now he's got to understand that I snatched up part of his soul, too.

He's looking for me now. It took a while for it to start at his brain. But it finally kicked in. He won't go thirty seconds without sneaking another peek at my face. Later on, when it gets down to crunch time, I'll be looking for Mustard. And there's nowhere to hide out there. If they're still ahead, I'll be catching his eye every two or three seconds. And if he doesn't dump enough points on his own, that'll wreck his concentration.

I want this fifth championship more than anything. But if I got to lose to Greene, it won't be by more than those five points. That's for damn sure.

There goes Mustard again, turning his head to see how I'm standing. He's my little puppet now, and I'll pull at every string before it's over.

5

FAT ANTHONY CAME to J.R.'s wake. He looked me dead square in the eye when he walked through the door but never said a word to me.

"I'm sorry for your loss," Anthony told J.R.'s pops. "I hope they catch the bastard that did it, and give you five minutes alone with him before they slap the cuffs on."

I'd never heard Fat Anthony's voice that way before. It sounded straight from the heart, without any hustle to it. But Stove wasn't closing his eyes on anybody. And after Fat Anthony left, he got me alone in the corner.

"You don't see that side of Anthony too much, or maybe he's just that good a liar," said Stove. "I know lots of people get good at hiding the truth when they have to."

I didn't know what to say, and I felt the back of my legs turn to rubber, staring down into Stove's chest.

Greene was at the wake, too. Only it was more like he put in a personal appearance. He came with two dudes from his posse and signed autographs outside the funeral home for almost fifteen minutes. Right before he got there, somebody delivered a big bunch of green flowers shaped like a dollar sign that nearly touched the ceiling. The words across it read FOREVER A GREENBACK. ALWAYS, J-GREENE AND YOUR TEAMMATES.

I could see in Stove's face how much he hated them. But lots of kids were blown away by those flowers. And they were grieving for J.R., too, so Stove let them stay right there.

Greene came up from behind and slipped an arm around Stove's shoulder.

"That's the way it is on these streets," said Greene. "The young trees fall too soon."

Then Greene went up to kneel at the casket. But he never took his dark glasses off, not even to look at J.R. Those are the same shades he's got on tonight.

Non-Fiction scores a basket, and Fat Anthony punches the air, mouthing off. "Keepin' it real, Non-Fiction!" he screams. "Keepin' it real!"

Players are moving all around me. Their eyes are burning with fire. I can see the fight inside every one of them, and how they'd tear somebody to pieces to win. Even kids who aren't tough on the street can turn into killers once they get a basketball in their hands. But it's not personal. It's something pure the game brings out in them. That's how it was with J.R. And I only wish that fuck would have stepped to him without that knife, in the middle of a tournament game, when J.R. was running hot, too. The Spanish curse words would have been flying from J.R.'s mouth, and I know it would have been somebody else's blood on the ground.

That's something I'd bet on.

We score another hoop. Then Fat Anthony makes the first sub of the game. The whole park's in shock because he brings this skinny old white guy off the bench. Maybe he's fifty years old. He comes jogging out in black canvas high-tops, like they wore back in the 1970s. Some people are even laughing, but kids on our squad know better.

Greene starts rhyming from the sideline—

"This old man, he tried to ball.
He forgot his Geri-tol. . . ."

"Take him serious. Don't give him any room out there," says Mitchell, shooting an invisible ball.

The guy's tag is Deadeye, because he can shoot the lights out cold. I'd seen him play before, and it doesn't matter how old he is. The dude's a window washer. He works all over the city and balls in every big yard. He carries a heavy wood ladder around all day, so his muscles are still strong. But he's a half step slower than anybody out here.

"Go home and tell your granddaddy to get off the couch. Deadeye's in the game," says Acorn. "He's wearin' number fifty-one, and that's his age."

I step over to guard him before anybody else does, like I was pulled there by a magnet.

The first time Deadeye touches the ball, I lay off him just a foot. He launches a long one-handed shot that probably nobody else would have took.

"Swish!" cries Acorn. "The old dog's teachin' the kiddies new tricks. Make it nine to six, Greenbacks."

I turn around and Fat Anthony's looking right at me.

Then Deadeye flashes me a smile, and most of his front teeth are missing.

I walk up court slow, pounding the rock. I can see Stove out of one eye, and out of the other, Deadeye playing defense on me. I can go by his wrinkled ass anytime I want. But I don't. Instead, I see somebody open down low, so I pass it inside.

The kid puts up the shot, and misses it bad.

Non-Fiction works the ball to Deadeye, way on the outside. I'm not going to give him an inch this time. But before I can get up on him, he lets one fly from downtown.

My hand falls in front of his face, and I follow the shot in his eyes. The whole crowd goes zoo, so I know he hit it. And I can feel the energy in the park start to change against me.

A couple of summers back, J.R. and me were playing one-on-one in the park when Stove showed up with some older guy. He was tall and thin, with a high-pitched voice.

"I want you boys to meet the Wrecker," said J.R.'s pops. "He used to live on this court, till he moved down south."

"Did you get that slick tag from knocking down houses, Mister?" asked J.R. with a smart mouth.

I thought his pops was going to dropkick J.R. across the park for being disrespectful. But the Wrecker broke out laughing and answered, "No, son. But I could *build* a house underneath the basket I was playin' defense on."

"Great! Let's play two-man," I said. "Young guns against the senior citizens."

The Wrecker didn't want to play at first. But J.R.'s pop almost begged him to.

"Just to shut their mouths for a while, so I can have some peace and quiet," said Stove. "You don't understand how they think they're all that."

We took the ball first and didn't think there was any way we could lose. Then J.R.'s pops stood over in the corner of the court with both hands in his pockets, like the Wrecker would beat us by himself.

"I'll stand here till it's over," said Stove with some real attitude.

I wouldn't go easy, even with it one-on-two. I made a move like I was going to shoot, then passed the ball to J.R. alone under the basket. But the Wrecker took one giant step inside. And the second the ball left J.R.'s hand, he slammed it across the court, all the way to the fence.

The *thud* echoed through the park, and the Wrecker and Stove just stayed quiet, waiting for one of us to bring the ball back.

I knew right then that we were in trouble. Only I wouldn't let myself believe it.

Next, I dribbled the ball up top and faked a pass to J.R. Then I headed for the hoop with a full head of steam. I stopped on a dime, and the Wrecker flew past me a step. I floated up a shot as high as I could. But the Wrecker wound up his long right arm and sent the ball flying over the fence into the street.

J.R. and me just looked at each other, and neither one of us would move for it.

"I'll get the ball. You two stay here and think about how good you are," cracked J.R.'s pops.

Soon as Stove left, J.R. and me nodded our heads to the Wrecker and bolted out the other end of the park. We could hear Stove calling after us from the street, but we wouldn't turn back around.

Acorn gave that guy the perfect tag—because he could wreck any confidence you had in your game. I tried to stay out of Stove's sight for the next couple of days. Only it was worse for J.R., because he had to go home.

But I was just a kid back then. I don't take any more lessons from old-timers. I do the schooling now. And I don't care that Deadeye's Fat Anthony's boy. I'm about to make him look stupid out here.

I blow past Deadeye, like his high-tops were nailed to the ground. I let go a wide-open jumper. It feels perfect. Only the ball goes halfway down into the rim, before it rattles back out.

"Damn!" I scream, slapping both my thighs.

Fat Anthony probably thinks I missed that shot on purpose, and that makes it even worse.

On defense, I'm all over Deadeye, and won't even let him touch the rock. Then one of our kids slaps the ball loose, and it rolls right in front of me. A pile of players dive for it. It's all arms and legs. But before I can grab it, the ball bounces off some kid's knee, right to Deadeye. He's standing by himself, and he buries the shot.

"Dead-*eye*! Dead-*eye*!" cheers the crowd.

"The old man's cookin' with gas!" hollers Acorn. "Non-Fiction takes the lead, ten to nine."

Mitchell's calling for a time-out. But I can't hold back. I get my hands on the ball and take off for the other basket. Most of our guys are headed for the bench, and it's like I'm going one-on-five.

Two white jerseys mug me, and we're fighting for the ball.

Hamilton runs over, yanking one of them away.

Then Stove grabs hold of me from behind as the sound from his whistle nearly splits my eardrums.

I rip the rock away from the last dude, and Stove falls face-first on top of me. My eyes are wide open, looking straight into his. Everything Stove's been chasing after me for is staring him in the face.

I shut my eyes tight. Then I jerk away with the ball, and Stove crashes to the cement. When I open my eyes, the spot where J.R. got killed is right between us. Stove sees it, too. One part even had to get painted over, where J.R.'s blood got in so deep it wouldn't wash out.

Mitchell runs out to us, screaming at Stove for not calling a foul.

I jump up and keep behind Mitchell, all the way back to the bench.

"Sorry, Coach," I say. "I didn't see you calling time-out."

"Then how'd you know that's what I was doing?" pops Mitchell, before he pulls the team around him.

Kids are jawing at me for running off on my own. Then Mitchell clears his throat, and everybody gets quiet.

"They're just on a run," says Mitchell. "Every good team makes one in a game. Let 'em get it out of their systems now."

"Somebody better wax grandpa's ass!" snaps Greene from over Mitchell's shoulder. "Mustard's the only one with any fight in him. It's supposed to be a war out there!"

"Mustard, you hear the crowd callin' that old dude's name?" asks Mitchell, without waiting for an answer. "Then go take back what he just stole from you!"

I walk onto the court with everything inside me ready to explode. Part of it isn't even basketball anymore. It's something dirty—something that hates me, and I hate it right back. I want to stomp on it. The same way I want to stomp on that fuck for what he did to J.R.

Then everything inside me falls flat.

Deadeye's not on the court. He's sitting on the bench with his warm-ups on, like he's through for the game.

Anthony's wearing a fat grin, like he just played me

for everything. And if I had the money he paid me in my fist right now, I'd ram it through his teeth.

"Faggot Anthony and Dead Dick—two cowards that can't finish a fight. That's what they are," spits Greene.

Stove blows his whistle to start play, and I push myself up the court.

Stove

Anthony's got Mackey's attention too good, and that makes me want to puke. It's that damn bet. I know it. And I have to know if that had anything to do with my son.

Ever since I lost J.R., I've been catching sight of people's eyes. I want to look straight inside them for something more—something they might be keeping from me. Mackey's eyes were empty in front of mine. Maybe he's built up a wall so high, he's hiding the truth from himself. But I can't let it stay like that.

There's light flashing from eyes all around me. It's the kind of light that keeps me going. The kind that connects you to people—some of them you hardly know.

Then I hit a splinter of dark, and it's like getting punched in the gut out of nowhere. And there's no way of telling where it came from, or who might have slipped up, showing what's really inside.

6

A KID ON our squad sticks his hand in front of a pass. The ball hits the tip of his finger, dead on, and everybody hears the *pock* as it pops out of the socket.

He's screaming, holding his hand tight against his stomach. Lots of kids got their heads turned, probably feeling the pain shooting through their fingers, too.

Only it's worse for me.

I can still see J.R. twisting on the ground, and hear that one bad scream he let out when he first got stabbed.

It was the worst sound I'd ever heard. I wake up every morning with it tearing through my ears. And it hits me even harder when I'm at Rucker Park.

This was the one place I could sidestep everything that had me tight—my mom's husband, school, shorties, *everything.* Now I can't even open my eyes all the way here. I don't care how much paint they slap on that spot. It's still J.R.'s blood out there.

And I keep running over it with my kicks, like it's nothing to me.

"It's just a finger," says Greene. "Tape it up to the next one, or get me a kid off the bench with more heart!"

Mitchell subs for the kid and brings in Junkyard Dog.

"Here come the Dawg," announces Acorn, with the crowd barking.

Junkyard Dog's one of the toughest park players around. That's because he's naturally mean, and even kids on his own team give him extra space. But it's a different game with refs on the court. If Dog misses a wide-open shot, or his man scores on him first, he's going to pound somebody for sure. He can pick up two or three fouls inside a hot minute. That's why he's not playing for Fat Anthony. He can't control himself. And it's not just basketball—he's the same way on the street. But he's that tough, too, and that counts for a lot in a war like this.

"You keep a tight leash on Dog," Fat Anthony calls to Hamilton.

Fat Anthony's working Hamilton like he's got the

only whistle on the court. Stove's almost invisible to him. That's because he's got too much time around Fat Anthony to be played like that.

I wish I could pretend Stove wasn't here, too.

And that everything I did never happened.

Non-Fiction scores. Then I come back and nail a long jumper in my man's face. The next time I touch the rock, Hamilton blows his whistle, pointing at me. There's a streak of blood on the ball that comes off onto my fingers. Only I don't have a cut. Players are eyeing each other up and down to see who it's coming from. But it's J.R.'s pops that's bleeding from the bottom of his hands. I guess he scraped them bad on the concrete when he fell on top of me.

Stove goes over to the scorer's table to get patched up.

I stare at the blood, and my hands start to feel like they're on fire. I shake them, trying to get the blood off. But it sticks. Then I press my fingers together hard, like I could make it all disappear by squeezing it down to nothing. But when I pull them apart, the blood's deeper into my skin, and shows my fingerprints clear.

It's the same blood that got J.R. born.

I just want it off of me.

"Try this!" says Mitchell, throwing me a towel.

I wipe my hands on it, but the blood won't all come

off. Stove's almost ready to go, and my hands are still burning.

Greene brings me over a bottle of water and pours it on my hands. I rub them together, and the water runs through my fingers onto the floor in a puddle. Then it soaks into the ground, the same way J.R.'s blood did.

"Get all that shit off," says Greene. "You need to keep a good grip on the ball."

I look at the bling hanging around Greene's neck and want to twist it so tight that he can't breathe. Then the next time he opens his mouth, nothing will come out.

Play starts up. We're ahead by two points, and I wish the game could finish right there. Then Fat Anthony would be off my back. I'd walk away with the trophy, and whatever I had left inside of me that I didn't sell.

My hands are aching. I touch the ball, and the shock runs up my arms. I can feel something between my hands and the rock. The blood's gone, but my hands still feel dirty. I wipe them across my jersey and shorts. Nothing helps.

Finally I put my head down and try to play through it. But that good feeling of a basketball in my hands is gone.

Junkyard Dog's got his man outmuscled down low. He flashes open through a crowd of players, and I dish him the rock quick. Dog snatches the pass and dunks it so hard over his man that he knocks him flat to the ground.

"That's the *In Your Face Disgrace Jam*," sounds Acorn.

The whole park's woofing.

Dog pulls both arms back and takes a running start at me. He slams his chest into mine to celebrate. My face is right up in his. Part of me wants to tell him how I'm really fucking our squad over. Then Junkyard Dog would wipe the floor with me like I deserve, instead of pounding chests together.

"You the Mustard, I'm the Dog!" he shouts.

But I never open my mouth back.

The guy who got dunked on is dragging his ass up court. Fat Anthony's all over him because he's got his head down.

"Don't you quit on *me*," sparks Anthony. "I'll put the bite on you ten times worse than Dog ever could!"

Quitting's a disease, and it's contagious, too. Coaches don't ever want to see you lose confidence. Fat Anthony will humiliate your ass in front of the whole park before he lets you put the idea of losing into other players' heads.

During the tournament one year, Fat Anthony's squad went into halftime ahead by almost forty points. So he put all his subs in to start the second half, and the other team went on a real run. But Fat Anthony never brought his starters back into the game, and Non-Fiction's lead got chewed down to ten points with just a minute left.

Anthony rode one of his subs up and down the court. J.R. and me were watching together. That sub was sweating more from hearing Fat Anthony than playing the game. He was shook bad. But the worst part was that he had a look on his face like the other team might really win.

There were just a couple of seconds on the clock when Fat Anthony finally sent somebody in for him. Only the kid didn't go back to the bench. He yanked his jersey over his head and handed it to somebody in the crowd. Then he walked out the side gate and headed down the boulevard, busted up inside.

I remember J.R. and me holding our sides from laughing so hard.

"He was like a kick-me dog," said J.R. "Fat Anthony planted a foot up his ass just by using his mouth."

"But Anthony's smart, too," I said. "You can bet another guy won't ever give up on him. That was a lesson for the whole yard to learn."

That kid used to play at Rucker Park all the time. But after that, he never came back.

Non-Fiction won the tournament that year. At the championship game, Fat Anthony fit that kid's jersey over an empty chair at the end of the bench for motivation.

Anthony pointed over to it and said, "Look at what's left of that quitting bastard! No arms! No legs! No heart! Nothing!"

Now I'm thinking that kid got off lucky. He only lost his pride for a little bit and bounced before Fat Anthony could cut a bigger piece out of him. I bought Anthony's rap from top to bottom. And it cost J.R. everything.

Maybe that kid's in the crowd right now laughing at me, or crying.

That's right, stick it to them. It all belongs to us—everything out here.

"You're wearin' my name! Never lose my name, boyz!"

From a group home to having groupies. Just crown me fuckin' king. I'll free-style my ass off right here, and spit out a brand-new hit.

"I flow like a river.

They call me Rhyme Giver.

From the North to the South, I keep on blazin' with my mouth."

It's like printing money with my own picture on it. Sharp tongue, sharp clothes, sharp car, sharp women—that's my game. All smooth and easy like. Just nobody better cross me—sharp teeth, too.

Anthony thought he could pull a fast one on me and set one of his rats loose in my house. But a snake can swallow a rat whole anyday. That's nature—the way God made it. Everybody's got their price. Buy and sell. That's the whole world.

7

NON-FICTION MAKES a steal, and Stove sprints up court, following the play. He's headed straight for me. Only I don't move my feet. My knees lock tight and I hold my ground. Stove hasn't looked up yet. So I stick out my chest, like nothing he's got could make a dent in me. Then I close my eyes, waiting for the hit. But all I feel is the wind coming off Stove as he runs by.

I catch back up, but Stove isn't looking at me. His eyes are glued to the game.

"*Baloncesto es todo*," J.R.'s mom used to tease Stove. "Our apartment could be on fire, and as long as your family wasn't inside, you wouldn't take that stupid whistle out of your mouth till the game was over."

Right after she died, Stove almost lived at Rucker Park with J.R. and me. I guess neither one of them wanted to be home without her. But it was different after J.R. got killed. Stove didn't set foot inside Rucker Park till tonight. And I didn't want to be here, either.

When the ball's in my hands, I'm in control. I move left, and everybody goes with me. Then I dribble right, and kids shift back that way, too. It's all at my speed, and the rhythm I want to play. But deep down, I don't have a handle on anything. My mind's racing in every direction, and my heart keeps switching sides.

I shake the dude playing defense on me and get into the clear. Then I raise up to take a jumper. The dude comes flying back at me, waving a hand across my face.

"You got nothin'," he says as I let the ball go.

I've heard crap like that all my life, and it never threw me off. But this time it sinks in, and the shot *clangs* off the iron rim.

"I make the loud noises here, Mustard!" screams Greene. "You stick to that sweet *swish* sound!"

I wish Greene had stayed in the studio. That he never came to Rucker Park, and that Fat Anthony never talked me into any of his bullshit.

The morning after our first tournament game— almost a week before J.R. got killed—I was riding high from Acorn blessing me with my tag. I got to the park by eight thirty, but nobody else was around. So I laid out on the benches and closed my eyes. There was nothing I needed to hide from then. There was just the orange light from the sun sneaking under my eyelids, and a warm feeling on my face.

That's when I heard a car door slam.

"Looky here, it's Hold the Mustard—just got born last night," said Fat Anthony. "Can't your family afford you a bed?"

Fat Anthony took a brand-new basketball from his trunk and pumped it full of air. Then he tossed it over the fence to me.

"I'll be right with you," he said, making a call on his cell.

When he finished, Fat Anthony came inside the park and started feeding me passes. I must have canned eighteen out of twenty shots from across the circle.

"We need to make some money together," said Anthony, straight out.

I knew everything Stove said about him was true. But Fat Anthony had been connected to some of the best players to ever come out of Rucker Park. He helped them pick the right college and stayed tight with them money-wise while they were still in school and poor. Then he got them a real agent to make a run at the pros, or to play somewhere in Europe.

Maybe I wasn't going to be the best college player in the country and walk right into the pros. Maybe I was going to be somewhere in the middle and have to scrap for a shot at playing anywhere. Then having Fat

Anthony in my corner could be big—real big.

"You know J.R.'s got some real talent, too. But his father thinks I'm some kind of *bandido*," said Fat Anthony. "Maybe he's been looking at too many WANTED posters down at the post office where he works."

And we both laughed out loud at Stove.

"You don't have any problems with winning all your games, do you?" asked Anthony. "You're okay with winning them the *right way*?"

I knew he was talking about betting on our games, and me making sure my squad won by less than the point spread. I'd heard enough about Fat Anthony to know I had to trade something for him pushing me to the pros.

"I'll put you on the payroll for the game coming up this week," said Fat Anthony, digging out a wad of cash from his front pocket.

He dropped five hundred bucks into my hand.

I thought Fat Anthony was talking crazy. Non-Fiction could play with any team. They might even beat us, straight up. How could I keep the score down against a squad that good? Who would bet on the Greenbacks and spot Fat Anthony a bunch of points? It didn't make any sense.

"Yeah, but who's gonna give—?" I said, before Anthony stopped me cold.

"That's for me to worry about. Not you," he said.

To me, it wasn't like dumping the game at all. I could still play to win.

I'd never held that much money at one time before. And I started thinking—*If there were enough paydays like this one, maybe I could move out on my own and get clear of my mom's husband. I could sidestep all that fighting and yelling and visit Mom when he wasn't around.*

So I swallowed hard. Then I closed one hand tight around the bills and laid the ball into the basket with the other.

A delivery kid rode through on a bike and handed Fat Anthony a brown paper bag.

"I called and ordered us breakfast," said Fat Anthony. "You hungry, Mustard?"

We sat on a bench, eating bacon-egg-and-cheese sandwiches. I told him everything I wanted to do in basketball, right up to the pros. Anthony listened to every word while he stuffed his face with food.

When he was full, Fat Anthony burped loud and said, "I can handle all of that for you. But first comes the game this week. I'll let you know how many points you can win by."

After a while, the park started to fill up with players, and they were almost ready to choose sides for the first pickup game. I was still sitting with Anthony when somebody said, "I got Hold the Mustard for my team."

That got my blood really pumping.

My shorts didn't have any pockets, so I stuffed the money down into a sock. I stepped onto the court and turned back to look at Anthony. Only he made out like he didn't know me anymore.

Fat Anthony never had to tell me how much I could win by. I was there when he suckered Greene into spotting him those five points.

And maybe he suckered me, too.

Junkyard Dog snaps down a rebound. He swings both elbows around to clear out space, and this dude called Kodak crashes to the floor.

But Dog hardly touched him.

Kodak took a flop, pretending he got nailed. He even let loose the air in his lungs with a *huh* before he fell.

Hamilton calls the foul right away.

"He should get an Academy Award for acting that good!" shouts Mitchell.

They call that dude "Kodak" because he looks like he's always posing for a picture, trying to fake out the refs. Stove didn't fall for it, just Hamilton did.

"The ASPCA needs to put Dog's ass to sleep," hollers Fat Anthony. "He's vicious out there!"

Hamilton's checking to see if Kodak's okay. But Stove isn't worried a bit.

"I think this one's gonna be all right," says Stove, leaning in.

Dog's red hot over the call. He keeps barking at the refs till Stove's got no choice, and hits him with a technical. Then Kodak steps to the foul line and knocks down the free throw.

"Damn Dog! Don't give points away!" pops Greene.

On the next play, Junkyard Dog clocks somebody for real, and both refs make the call.

"I'm not gettin' cheated no more!" growls Dog. "You wanna make calls? I'll give you somethin' to call."

Non-Fiction drops home two more foul shots. It's down to a three-point lead for us, with time running out in the first half.

Mitchell's talking to Junkyard Dog from the sideline in an easy voice. I can see that Dog's ready to blow. And if Greene sets him off with his big mouth, maybe that'll save me. Dog could cost us enough points on fouls that I can play for real. Then maybe he'll tear Greene a new one, and Anthony, too, before the cops haul him off.

There's less than a minute left. Mitchell wants me to hold the ball for the last shot of the half. I dribble around in little circles. Then I stand still and eye the guy guarding me, while I pound the rock.

The guy's zeroed in on my midsection. A dribbler can fake you out a hundred different ways. His shoulders and arms can go right, while his legs go left. But he's not going anywhere without his stomach.

"Basketball and life are the same—you got to have it in your stomach to get somewhere. And you can't go anywhere without taking your stomach with you," Stove once told J.R. and me. "You've got to be able to stomach everything you do, or else it'll eat away at you from the inside."

The wind kicks up and raises goose bumps on my sweaty skin.

I start my move with ten seconds to go, and don't even bother to fake. I jet past my man. But before I can turn the corner, a second defender cuts me off. He jumps sky high with his arms and legs spread wide in front of me. I'm heading out-of-bounds. There's no J.R. to save my ass. So I leave my feet, and just throw the ball up to the basket.

My head's turned the other way, and I can't see the hoop. But I hear the sound of the rim being rocked, and the crowd explodes.

I look back and Junkyard Dog's standing under the iron. He just jammed my pass home, and is pounding his chest like he's King of the Hill. Everybody's all over him, and kids are slapping *my* back, too. But I can't celebrate anything.

"Who let the Dawg out?" Acorn calls to the crowd.

"Who? Who? Who?" they shout back in rhythm.

Off Dog's dunk, we're up 42 to 37.

The game's half over.

I'm that much closer to winning the championship.

And the bet between Greene and Fat Anthony is dead even.

8

HALFTIME'S WHEN J.R. and me would talk for real. We'd listen to the coach go on about what he wanted to do. But we'd always catch each other's eye, and wait for him to finish. Then we'd put our heads together and come up with all kinds of plans to win games on our own.

I never trusted anybody more than J.R. He could see things clear and would always tell me the truth. Even if I was playing like crap, he'd say it to my face and wouldn't cut me any slack.

That's what I was worried about most when I took Fat Anthony's money—hiding it from J.R. He might have known I was holding back on playing my best from the beginning. Then he would have been all over me for dogging it on the court.

At least J.R. never had to see me dump a single play.

There are no locker rooms at Rucker Park. Everything's out in the open, so you got to keep yourself in check. Ballers don't hide under a helmet or sit in a dugout. You play in shorts and a tank top, and people can see every muscle twitch. So you can't let on that you're tired or pissed off, or the other team will use that to prop themselves up. You got to hide all of that and learn how to front.

Our starters are still standing. Nobody wants to sit for a half hour and have their muscles go stiff. Kids got towels over their heads, too, so they won't lose that good sweat they got going. Once you stop sweating, everything inside you goes cold. Then you got to start up again, and find another flow, like it's a brand-new game.

Before Mitchell can say a word, Greene gets in front of the team.

"*Blow. Their. Asses. Out. The. Park!*" shouts Greene, one word at a time. "Understand? No mercy! Run up the score on these fools. I want this game to be talked about forever."

Everybody knows about Greene's bet.

I figure kids on my team will try to add to the score in the last minute, and maybe catch a few bucks from Greene for it. So I might be working against that, too. Part of me can't wait to fuck Greene on the score. If we win, I want to see him have to fake a smile, holding the championship trophy, because we didn't cover the points.

When Greene's finished, he goes off to act like a star with the crowd. That's when Mitchell drops his shoulder, like he's going to throw a punch at us, and starts his own speech.

"Guess what? Non-Fiction thinks they're tougher than we are. That's the only reason they're still in this game," says Mitchell, grilling our guys. "And maybe they're right, too. Maybe we're better ballplayers, but they can whip our ass in a street fight!"

Coaches use that kind of talk all the time to get their team stoked. I don't think any of our kids really bought it. But the crowd behind our bench can hear every word, and they start making noises at us, like we're pussies. None of us can stomach that shit. I see in kids' faces how they're ready to run over anybody who'd get in front of us. So I guess Mitchell got what he wanted.

Non-Fiction's pulled so tight around Fat Anthony that I can't see him. But I know he's going off with his mouth, because his players are all stone silent, nodding their heads.

The court's filled with little kids putting on a dribbling show, and Stove's watching from the sideline.

Some of those squirts aren't even big enough to reach the basket with a shot. But they dribble like they were born with a ball in their hands.

One time, J.R. and me saw a TV special on Pistol Pete. He was one of the greatest ball handlers ever. Pistol Pete was a skinny white dude from the South whose pops was a basketball coach. When Pistol was a kid, he never went anywhere without the rock. He was the first one to get to the yard in the morning, and the last to leave at night. For hours every day, he'd work on his handle. There's even a film of him dribbling out the window, sitting in the backseat of his pops's car.

"Nobody in my family's got any wheels," complained J.R., after we saw that show. "But I don't care. I'm takin' a ball with me everywhere, till I get a handle like Pistol!"

So we snuck a ball into the movies inside a gym bag—the same as Pistol Pete. We both sat at the end of a row and took turns dribbling during the flick. First, some girl cursed us out over the noise we were making. Then her boyfriend came over. He was diesel from the floor up and threatened to slap the shit out of us. J.R. and me just kept our mouths shut and put the rock away. After that, we quit on the idea of copying Pistol Pete.

Before the last little kid leaves the court, Stove grabs

him by the waist and lifts him up over his head. Then the kid shoots the ball into the basket. And I think about how many times Stove probably lifted J.R. like that when he was small.

Greene gets the mike from Acorn, and one of his beats starts playing low over the PA system.

"I see the city sent a whole mess of po-lice officers here tonight. And we all know how a whole mess of po-lice can just make a bigger mess out of things," says Greene, laughing at his own joke. "But that's the way it is when you throw a party in the hood. The city's got to keep both eyes on you. Frisking everybody that comes in the joint, like the park ain't yours no more. See, they got to watch you close. They're afraid you'll all get together and figure a way to dig yourselves out the hole they got you in.

"Now, just think about the word 'po-lice' for a minute. The 'po' part is for poor people. You know like, 'I'm so *po* I got to run my game to survive.' The l-i-c-e part is for lice, like the bugs that get into your scalp. So po-lice are just bugs in the scalps of poor people. That's why they're always in your hair.

"But I found a way out of that trap when I hit it big in the music business. I got myself a shitload of money, and I wasn't *po* no more. Then I went out and bought myself a big stick—the only kind they respect. I'm not talkin' 'bout a two-by-four. No. No. I got myself an ass-kickin' lawyer to whomp 'em good with. And I wrote a rap about it.

"Pump up the volume on that beat so I can spit this proper.

"Rucker Park, check out this rhyme—

"Boom Boom Boom, it's time for Cochran,
Boom Boom Boom, it's time for Cochran,
Boom Boom Boom . . .

I was chillin' in my ride, cruisin' up Lex.
Had Shorty in my lap, she was bobbin' for my Rolex.
Saw that punk MC always stealin' my rhymes.
Dropped Shorty at the corner and pulled the Tek-9.

That's when the cops rolled up on me,
like it was Giuliani-Time.

Boom Boom Boom, it's time for Cochran,
Boom Boom Boom, it's time for Cochran,
Boom Boom Boom . . .

They slapped the cuffs on me.
They tried to get rough with me.
But I wasn't havin' it, so they took a pass.

Rucker Park Setup

Now I gotta limp to court 'cause my foot's
stuck up some cop's ass.

They say I resisted but their words is twisted.

Boom Boom Boom, it's time for Cochran,
Boom Boom Boom, it's time for Cochran,
Boom Boom Boom . . .

The state can indict me.
The DA, she can bite me.
I won't never cop a plea.
They don't know how to take me.
All they want to do is break me,
'Cause I'm a gangster with a capital G.
Only one thing I want to know—
How come the judge's robes are blacker than me?

Boom Boom Boom, it's time for Cochran,
Boom Boom Boom . . .

They can't stand a brother my age
makin' more than the minimum wage.

Boom Boom Boom, it's time for Cochran,
Boom Boom Boom . . .

I'm not showin' up with some legal aid.
I got a lawyer gets paid, big-time.

Boom Boom Boom, it's time for Cochran,
Boom Boom Boom . . .

A jury of my peers?
They're all upstate doin' years.

Boom Boom Boom, it's time for Cochran,
Boom Boom Boom . . .

Johnny shows 'em no mercy,
'Cause the cops don't curtsy.

Boom Boom Boom, it's time for Cochran,
Boom Boom Boom . . .

Black enough to fit the description,
Got a pocketful of green for the right prescription.

Boom Boom Boom, it's time for Cochran,
Boom Boom Boom, it's time for Cochran,
Boom."

9

THE CROWD GOES wild for Greene's rap, stamping their feet till the ground starts to tremble. But none of the cops are clapping, and I know they'd like to shove that mike up Greene's ass for what he said.

Stove's eyes are down on the ground while Greene takes his bows.

"Just gimme your gun, Sergeant. I'll shoot that asshole myself!" Acorn tells the cop closest to the court, not even caring if Greene hears him.

"He's got no respect! No respect for how this game gets put on!" Fat Anthony yells to Acorn.

Acorn takes the mike and waits for the crowd to quiet down.

"We support artistic expression in the community, so props to J-Greene," says Acorn in a cold voice. "But we also want to recognize that we couldn't have this game without help from the city and the police department. So a special thanks to them as well!"

We walk onto the court and start to warm up. That's when Acorn goes behind the scorer's table and unwraps the gold championship trophy. He pulls back the plastic and the brown paper from it, with everybody watching. Then he puts the trophy on top of the scorer's table for both teams to drool over.

The trophy never gets put out till the second half because that's when the championship game gets won. You can't get lazy and coast to the title—not at Rucker Park. You have to scrap till the last second on the clock to go home with something that important. Just because you smack the other team in the mouth first and get a lead, doesn't mean they're going to quit. If you don't keep fighting hard, they could come back and knock *you* out.

"Four times I took that trophy home," Fat Anthony hollers at his squad. "And I tell you, sweet five is in the air tonight. Take a deep breath with me, everybody! Can you smell it? I said, 'Can you *smell* it?'"

Mitchell brings us together at our bench. He's been laid-back for most of the tournament, but his eyes are locked on ours, and he's breathing fire now.

"Boys, you see that trophy? I played pro ball in New York for eight years, and maybe you think *that's* special.

But I never got a chance at winning Rucker Park!" snorts Mitchell. "You know who else never got that chance? J.R. That got ripped away from him with everything else. J.R. would have given anything to run up and down this court, all out! So don't any of you dog it for a second. Play with everything you got 'cause J.R.'s runnin' with you out there. I guarantee it! Now take one more look at that trophy, and make damn sure the next time you see it, Non-Fiction's not carryin' it off the court!"

Kids are bouncing up and down, and that speech has got my feet moving, too. Only I know that J.R.'s not out here with us. He's at my crib, standing inside his good kicks, waiting on me to set things right.

Acorn's telling the crowd who Holcombe Rucker was, and how the tournament helps get kids scholarships to colleges all over the country.

"Holcombe called this game the 'Ghetto Express' 'cause it got our kids into places nobody thought they could ever go," says Acorn. "But he believed in more than basketball. He wanted our kids to study once they got into a school. And he didn't just talk it, he walked it. Holcombe Rucker enrolled in college himself at thirty-five, and left the Parks Department to become a New York City teacher."

History was J.R.'s favorite school subject. He even got an A on a paper he did on Holcombe Rucker one time. His pops would bring him home stamps from the post office with pictures of people we'd never heard of. Then J.R. would look up what they did. And every time somebody talked to us about a college, J.R. asked if he could study history there.

I step onto the court and take one long breath. I look straight up, so I don't have to face anybody. The stars are just starting to shine in the sky. I can't tell one from the next, or which one J.R.'s mom taught him how to wish on. Then I feel the pressure building up inside my chest, till I can't take it anymore. So I bring my eyes back down to everything around me. I empty my lungs and start to breathe again.

Both squads switch hoops for the second half. Now we're shooting at the basket Non-Fiction was gunning for, and guarding the one we were trying to score at. And if I closed my eyes and spun around in circles, it wouldn't matter which basket I was facing when I opened them again. I still got work to do for both sides.

We won the opening tap, so Non-Fiction gets the ball to start this half. They inbound the rock and come right at us. Fat Anthony calls out a set play. Their ball handler comes free around a pick. He drives for the hoop and lets go of a shot. Then out of nowhere, one of our kids pops up and slams the ball back down his throat.

"Dinner has been served!" crows Acorn over the

crowd. "And the menu reads, SPALDING RUBBER—OFFICIAL SIZE AND WEIGHT."

Without thinking, I turn to J.R.'s pops. I bring my hand up to my forehead and wipe away the sweat. Stove taught J.R. and me that move as a salute to a monster blocked shot.

"Wilt Chamberlain was over seven feet tall. He was the most famous player in the world and even scored a hundred points by himself in an NBA game," Stove told us maybe fifty times. "But a bald-headed guy off the street named Jackson stuck Chamberlain's shot to the backboard in the tournament. It sent chills up my spine to see. But Jackson didn't whoop it up or anything. He just wiped the sweat off his head, like it was nothing."

A park player pinned Chamberlain's shot and didn't crack a smile. That's something special. So anytime we saw a block that good, J.R., his pops, and me would wipe the sweat from our heads, too, out of respect for what that dude Jackson did.

But Stove's hands are down at his side. He's looking at me like I lost my mind. That he couldn't celebrate anything with me, not after I fed him that bullshit story about how J.R. got killed.

I hate the way Stove treats me now, like he's waiting for me to step up. I wish he'd just slap me in the mouth and call me a liar. That way I could hate him, too.

Non-Fiction scores a basket, and I walk the ball back up court. Fat Anthony's staring right at me, and Stove's looking at Anthony and me together. For a second, I can't juggle anything else inside my head except the two of them.

I go to plant my foot, but the ground isn't there.

That's when I see a white jersey flying at me. I try to get my balance back, but I can't. The guy's right on top of me. I see his hands flash past mine. He picks my pocket clean and streaks the other way with the ball. I'm left there frozen in front of everybody, with nothing.

"Lord! Lord! Call the cops! There's a thief in the park!" blasts Acorn.

I hear the guy's footsteps going the other way. He's long gone. I only turn back around to chase him because I have to. And I won't look up to watch him score.

Our lead's down to one point, and Greene's having a shit fit on the sideline.

"Mustard, use the sight God gave you!" screams Greene, lowering his shades so I can catch a glimpse of his eyes.

I never spent a dime of Fat Anthony's money. It wasn't like I could throw a party without J.R. asking how all that cheddar got into my pockets. So I kept the cash in my clothes drawer, inside a balled-up pair of sweat socks.

Before J.R. got killed, I took the money out and counted it every night. I'd feel it in my fingers and snap the bills down into a pile, dreaming of my own apartment. Then I'd push the edges tight on every side, till it was all even. But I haven't undone those socks since.

I came home from J.R.'s funeral and locked the door to my room. I laid on the bed, playing catch up against the wall with those socks. I could feel what was inside them, and hear the sound of the money every time they hit. I wanted to bury those socks inside that wall. So I started throwing them harder and harder, till my arm went numb. But I couldn't break through, and they just kept bouncing right back.

Even my mom's husband came to the funeral, and didn't say shit to me that whole morning. But after we got home, I could hear his mouth starting up from the hall.

"Your son's got too much free time on his hands," he told Mom. "All this basketball's nonsense. He needs to see how the world really is, and work."

I wanted to go out there and throw Fat Anthony's money in his face.

"Leave him alone!" Mom took up for me. "He's been through enough today!"

"I'm the one that supports this house! You don't tell me what to do!" he popped off at her.

So I charged off the bed and put my foot into the door, wishing it was his pathetic ass.

He got right up on the other side, screaming, "You'll never be man enough! Never!"

Then I slammed my fist against it where I figured his face was, squeezing that sock tight inside my other hand. But I was worried that bigmouth bastard was right—that maybe in my whole life I'd never be man enough.

The next time I touch the ball, I don't even look at my teammates. I blow by my man, and can an open ten-footer. Then I strut back up court, like getting stripped by that guy didn't mean a thing to me.

Non-Fiction's running screen after screen, and we have to keep switching men on defense to pick up for each other. Somebody steps in front of me, blocking me off. So one of my teammates slides over to guard my man. Then I find the guy who's left open, and get my ass there quick. It's like playing musical chairs when you were a little kid. Only the music comes from your teammates talking.

"*Slide!*"

"*Pick!*"

"*He's mine!*"

"*I got your man!*"

Somebody else's man breaks free. I know I can get there. But I pretend I don't see him and stay glued to the guy I'm guarding instead.

"Credit that bucket to teamwork," says Acorn. "The tight-fitting parts of the Non-Fiction machine."

All the way up court, our kid's cursing himself out for getting bumped off his man and letting him score. And for me, listening to that kid's like getting kicked in the ass, over and over.

Fat Anthony's eyes are drilled into mine.

I just wish Anthony had some kind of X-ray vision. That way he could see inside me and know for sure exactly what I was going to do. Then I could look at his face and know how far I was willing to fuck my teammates.

10

NON-FICTION LOSES THE ball out-of-bounds, and I sprint to the sideline to put it back in play. Stove walks it over to me slow. He's squeezing the ball between his hands, like he could pop the air right out of it. Then he leans over to me so nobody else can hear.

"You're watching Fat Anthony more than your own coach," says Stove, handing me the rock. "What's up with that, Mackey?"

My brain goes blank, looking at him.

I watch Stove slice the air with his hand as he starts to count. I've got five seconds to get the ball inbounds. There's a kid wide open in front of me, waiting.

"Three," says Stove, slicing the night air again.

Only I can't let go. I lost my best friend *and* my second pops.

"Four," Stove says louder.

I see the panic on the kid's face and finally pass him the ball.

Then Stove stares me down all the way up the court.

He knows I'm down with Fat Anthony, and playing against the points. Stove's seen my game a million times and can probably tell every time I held back tonight. He must think I'm the worst little shit that ever lived. And he might have it figured out about J.R., too.

I take the ball and spin right, then left. I freeze the guy in front of me with a shoulder fake, leaving him flat-footed. A second defender rushes over to help out. That leaves a green jersey open in the corner, but I wouldn't pass the ball off now for anything. I drive to daylight through an open seam in the defense and lay the ball in the basket.

We're back up by five points, 50 to 45. And I shoot Stove a look, like he's wrong about everything.

Our next time up court, I let somebody else handle the rock. I run the baseline from side to side, making cuts and trying to get free. I lose my defender and take the pass. Then I put up a shot that bounces high off the front of the rim. My eyes are on the ball, and I go flying in for the rebound. I want to show Stove how hungry I am to win. But this kid named Bones throws his body in front of mine, blocking me off from the ball.

Bones is just six feet tall, and maybe a hundred and

seventy-five pounds when his jersey's soaked with sweat. But most of that is pure heart. He takes every good angle there is and sticks himself in front of anybody looking for a rebound. And once Bones gets square in front of you, it's like trying to get past a living, breathing wall.

Anytime I chose up sides at the park, I'd pick Bones for my squad, right after J.R. That way I wouldn't have to play against him.

"I hate when he drops his bony ass on me. It means too much to him. It's like he's tryin' to stop you from robbin' his house," J.R. complained one time after a pickup game. "But that's all Bones has got. He can't dribble. He can't shoot. He's not even a real player."

"The hell he ain't!" said J.R.'s pops. "Maybe Bones hasn't got half the raw talent of you or Mackey. But he's got what counts beating in his chest. *Juega con fuego*— he plays with that fire in his soul. The day you can get past what he throws down, you'll be something to deal with. And you can lift all the weights you want. You only get strong like Bones from the inside out."

Non-Fiction rebounds the rock. I'm tangled up with Bones, but I won't quit. I bang up against him with all my strength. I keep trying to get past, till Bones backs off to follow the ball the other way.

Stove's running a few steps up ahead, chasing the play. He balled with J.R. and me lots, till we were maybe fourteen. When Stove was on our squad he was all right, playing hard to win. But when he was going up against us, Stove would do whatever it took to stop us cold.

I remember when Stove got the transfer he was praying for and started delivering mail to our neighborhood. All summer, he'd move double-time through the morning. Everybody we knew got their mail by noon. Then Stove would ditch his cart and postman's shirt at Acorn's barbershop. He'd take a long lunch at the park and play pickup games in a white tee and those long gray pants with the black stripe down the side. He'd ball all the way up till four thirty, when he had to be back at the post office. And he was almost at the park as much as J.R. and me.

"It's like your pops is one of *us*," I told J.R. back then.

"Not to me," answered J.R. "Even when we're playing ball, he's still my pops."

Once, while he was still on post-office time, Stove sprained his ankle bad on the court. But he knocked out a plan on the spot. Real fast, he sent me to Acorn's for his shirt and cart. I ran full speed both ways. On the way back, I was hoping the cops wouldn't stop me, thinking I mugged a mailman. Then J.R. helped his pops limp back to his route, while I pushed the cart along next to them. When we got to the right corner, Stove called in from a pay phone for somebody to come get him. That way he could explain it better to his boss, like he'd got hurt on the job.

Now Stove's got himself a second wind. He's running as fast and strong as I've ever seen him. He's moving around the court like nothing could spot him from finding out the truth.

Junkyard Dog goes sky high over Bones for a rebound. Then he spins around and hits me with a pass. Up ahead, one of our kids is streaking alone to the basket. The ball's barely in my hands, and without thinking, I gun the pass to him. The kid catches the ball in stride and lays it in.

"Greenbacks by seven. That's the biggest lead of the game," announces Acorn.

I can hear Greene whooping it up, and part of me wishes I could dig myself a hole right here on the court. I'd jump in without thinking twice. Then I'd keep on digging straight down, till I came out in China.

Non-Fiction gets the ball inside and misses an easy layup. The rock just rolls around the rim and won't fall home, like there was an invisible lid on the basket. The guy who missed the shot's running back along the sideline, and Fat Anthony tries to kick him in the ass as he runs past.

I catch the ball with Kodak on me and back him down

under the basket. Then I slam both shoulders into him hard. Kodak goes down like a shot, even before I really hit him. I turn and score, waiting to hear a whistle. But Stove doesn't call me for the offensive foul, and neither does Hamilton.

The crowd lets out a long "*Ooooooooooh!*"

The hoop counts, and we go up by nine points.

Kodak's flat on his back, cursing.

Fat Anthony calls time-out so he can rip into Hamilton.

"*He* told you not to make those calls anymore. Ain't that right, Hambone?" screams Anthony, pointing at Stove. "You couldn't be that blind on your own! Nobody could!"

I walk back to our bench through all the noise and hear footsteps flying up from behind. Then I see his shadow come through mine on the floor, and I flinch.

It's Greene.

He wraps both arms tight around my stomach, and everything inside me freezes solid. Then Greene lifts me off the ground, and for a second, I forget how to breathe. My feet are reaching for the court, but it's not there. My head's raised back, and all I can see is the dark sky. It's like I lost my whole world. I'm stuck inside Greene's arms, and there's no place left for me anywhere.

Greene drops me back down. My heels hit hard, and

I feel a knot in my stomach where his hands shoved into me.

Everybody's running up to slap my back, but I won't take my eyes off of him.

"I love how you drilled that faker," says Greene. "Posers aren't entitled to shit in this world. I hope he never gets up off the fuckin' ground."

Stove

It's just a damn game, and I'm not going to make that call. Anthony can howl all he wants about it. I've got to push people to the limit if I'm going to find out who killed my son.

I don't care how many shots Mackey makes. I know he's in Anthony's pocket. I've seen Mackey have big games before. It didn't matter if it was in front of two hundred people in a high-school gym, or just a couple of kids playing pickup in the park. Mackey couldn't keep the light from pouring out of his eyes. He'd try hard to fight back a smile. But the muscles in his cheeks would always win out.

That's not Mackey out there. That's not even Hold the Mustard. It's some kid I hardly know trying to get out from under a mountain of shit.

I know how bad Mackey's hurting over J.R. He was there. He saw J.R. get stabbed to death. And after that, I don't know how Mackey could open his eyes again. He wants to push it as far away as he can. But I can't live with that. And until I find out for sure, I'm not gonna let Mackey out of my sight.

11

FAT ANTHONY'S SQUAD scores and cuts the lead to seven points. We fast-break the other way, and I get the ball in the middle of the court. I got a teammate open on each wing. Only one of them's this big, muscle-bound dude with hands like stones.

I look hard to my right. When the defense bites, I go to pass the ball off to my left. But I hesitate for a half-second, just enough to throw the big dude off stride. Then I push the ball into his palms, instead of laying it on his fingertips. He can't control the rock, and loses it out-of-bounds.

He slaps his hands together hard, and I can feel the sting.

"My bad!" he says, pointing at himself. "My bad!"

Mitchell and Greene are all over him for blowing an easy layup.

"That was a gift!" screams Mitchell. "You're either the kind of player who can win a championship or you're not!"

"No heart!" growls Greene. "He's hollow inside, like the Tin Man!"

And deep down, I know all of that should be for me.

The guy I'm guarding cuts across the court at full speed, and I'm right on his tail. I look up and see a shoulder from one of Fat Anthony's goons. But I can't slow down, and I plow straight into it, face-first.

I feel my jaw and neck snap back. My feet are off the floor, and a jolt shoots down my spine. My eyes go back inside my head, and for a second, there's nothing but bright light.

When my eyes start to focus again, J.R.'s standing right in front of me, wearing our high-school jersey. He's breathing hard, and the sweat's rolling down his brown face.

J.R. puts out a hand to pull me up off the court. I try to reach for it, but my arms are too heavy to lift.

I don't care if J.R. knows it all already. I have to tell him everything I did, and how I never meant for him to get hurt. I try to explain. But my mouth won't move.

J.R. bends all the way down to lift me up. That's when the feeling starts to run through my body again, and everything is all needles and pins.

Then my eyes start to focus for real.

It's Stove standing over me, not J.R.

"Mackey, are you all right?" asks Stove, tugging me to my feet. "Mackey?"

I turn around, looking everywhere for J.R. I know he's not really here. He's dead and buried. Still I look in every shadow and corner of Rucker Park for him just the same.

"Do you hear me, Mackey?" asks Stove, with his hands around my shoulders.

I back up out of his grip, taking a few shaky steps. And I don't know if the pain inside me is from the hit I took, or because I can't stand myself anymore.

Mitchell's there, too.

"I'm stayin' in the game, Coach!" I say.

He's flipped over me getting dropped like that.

"That's not a foul! It's a felony!" cracks Mitchell.

"You're right!" says Stove, who signals Anthony's goon for a flagrant foul, and throws him out of the game.

The crowd boos the shit out of that guy as he walks off the court. But when he gets back to the bench, Anthony gives him a pound, like he did his job perfect.

I walk to the foul line for two free throws, and Fat Anthony's eyes stab mine.

That bastard had his boy knock me flat. I guess that

was supposed to be some kind of reminder. But Anthony doesn't own me, and *he* better remember that.

I set my feet at the edge of the foul line, and Stove sends me the ball. Then I take a deep breath and look back to where I saw J.R. Only that part of the court is empty.

The foul line's called the charity stripe because nobody guards you or waves a hand in your face. It's like they're giving those points away, so you're supposed to make every one.

Kids can knock down free throws in practice all day long. But in a game, it's a different story. Never mind the crowd or the pressure; sprinting up and down the court can zap your legs good. Then you get tired and don't follow through on the shot.

"There are plenty of excuses for missing free throws," Stove always told J.R. and me. "But that's all they are—excuses. Big-time players make those shots, no matter what."

So every time Stove saw us walking out of the park exhausted, he'd challenge J.R. and me to make two straight free throws before we left.

"I can't figure out if your pops is tryin' to make us better players or if he just wants to torture us," I'd say to J.R.

"Either way, it's still basketball," he'd always answer.

But it isn't just basketball anymore. Not for me. And maybe I can't afford to make both free throws.

I clear the air from my lungs. Then I raise up and release the ball. It's right on line, but I can feel that my stroke's off a hair.

The shot rims the basket, and spins out.

My teammates lined up along the foul line clap for me anyway. But I can hear Fat Anthony clapping the loudest.

"This is our time, Non-Fiction," says Anthony.

I step back off the foul line and shake loose every part of me. You never stay at the line after a missed shot, because you know something's off. Then I go to reset myself, and Stove walks the ball out to me.

"You could make these free throws blindfolded if you wanted," Stove says low.

J.R. would think up different games when we practiced foul shots. We'd see who could hit the most in the row, or the best out of twenty. Underhanded, one-handed—it didn't matter. We'd do anything to keep it from getting boring.

Fooling around in the park one day, I made three straight with my eyes closed. J.R. couldn't come close to matching that, and I bragged about it for a week. Then Stove showed up at the park with a blindfold.

"This will separate the men from the boys," said

Stove. "Maybe we oughtta make it interesting, like the loser runs laps."

"No way!" said J.R. "Pops, you should have seen Mackey nail those free throws with his eyes shut."

I told J.R. he was scared, and kept dissing him till he bet me. I pushed it up to ten laps around Rucker Park, with the loser skipping all the way and clucking like a chicken.

Stove tied the blindfold on J.R. first and stood him even with the rim. He handed him the ball, and J.R. reached out for it like a blind man. But J.R. started knocking down free throws, one after another. I was in shock and felt my stomach start to turn.

"Really! That one went in, too?" asked J.R. in a surprised voice.

He made eight out of ten, and I couldn't say a thing.

I stepped to the foul line and swallowed hard. Then Stove tied the blindfold on me. Only it was a fake, and I could see right through it.

They were both rolling on the floor, laughing.

"¡Qué lástima!" said Stove, pointing at me. "Poor chicken! *Cluck! Cluck!*"

Finally I had to start laughing, too. I never expected something like that from them. But they played me good.

Now I'm standing at the foul line with everybody

watching. I close my eyes, and there's nothing but dark. Then I open them again, and the only thing I let myself see is the front lip of the rim. The shot's perfect out of my hand, and settles through the net without even touching iron.

Non-Fiction misses their next shot. But Bones out-fights everybody for the ball and taps it in. Then he turns his shoulders sideways and slips out through the crowd of players.

We're up 55 to 49.

Fat Anthony thought Bones got fouled on that play. He's all over Hamilton about it and won't let up. Hamilton gives him a long look and a chance to back off. But Fat Anthony doesn't take it.

"You can't miss calls like that, Ham!" hollers Anthony. "What the fuck were you looking at?"

That's when Hamilton puts one hand on top of the other and hits Fat Anthony with a *T*.

Fat Anthony

I needed to pop Ham's cork. I can't let him ref the rest of this game with a hard-on for me. Let him get it out of his system now and smack me with a technical.

"I was wrong to say that, Mr. Hamilton. From now on, nothing but basketball."

That'll soften him towards my team down the stretch.

But I got one more ace in the hole that nobody knows about. And I'll give the signal for it to kick in any minute.

That's it, send Mustard to the line to shoot the technical.

The prick. When I tap a kid, it should be a done deal from the start. I shouldn't have to sweat out a minute of this crap. Mustard's playing it from the front end. He needs to hear everybody cheering his name before he gets himself too dirty. But he didn't want to be the hero when his best friend got killed. He doesn't even have the guts to say what really happened. I know he's feeling that. So he puts himself on a tightrope with my money and sees how far he can go without looking down. All because he's a spineless little nobody with something to prove.

"Ha! Good miss, Mustard! Good miss!"

I thought Mustard being a coward was going to make this bet easy. I should have known better. Murders go down in a heartbeat. It takes two hours to dump a game. And that's too much time for a kid to think.

12

THERE'S A LIGHT shining off that trophy, and it catches my eye. J.R. and me used to joke that it was more beautiful than any shorty we knew. Every year we'd watch that trophy as much as the second half of the championship game.

We'd won lots of trophies balling. So do most kids playing youth league. When you're young, they give you a trophy just for tying your kicks right. Then you get older, and the trophies start to mean something.

Some of the best players to throw down at Rucker Park never won a championship. Only one squad a year gets to hold that trophy, and they got to survive everything to do it.

"It's not just on the court," I told J.R. before the tournament started. "It's every step you take in this neighborhood. You never have to lower your head to anybody with that trophy behind you."

"It'll put me ahead of my pops at Rucker, too," said J.R. "And he's just gonna have to live with that."

Every inch of the dude on top of that huge trophy is covered in gold—his arms, his face, and the uniform he's got on. One arm is straight over his head, with a basketball in his hand. He's holding the rock up to the sky, like nobody could ever jump up high enough to slap it away.

Acorn only hands out one trophy right after the game—to show that a whole squad pulled together to win the championship. All the players take turns holding it in front of the crowd, even guys on the bench who never got into the game. Then later on, everybody gets a trophy of their own to keep.

"I got twenty-seven trophies on those two shelves in my room. But I wouldn't keep any of them next to the big one," said J.R., before this year's tournament started. "That's goin' on the top shelf by itself. All the others are gonna have to fit underneath. I don't care if I gotta push some into the closet."

"You got to. That's for the championship of all street ball. The rest of 'em are just kiddie toys," I said. "I don't know what I'd do with mine. Maybe I'd put it on a gold chain and wear it around my neck."

"Oh, shit! Rucker Park bling!" cracked J.R.

J.R. and me would have done anything to win that trophy. But now it's sitting right in front of me, and I'm holding back on my best game.

They'll give J.R.'s trophy to Stove for sure if we win.

I'd tell him how J.R. wanted to keep it on his top shelf. Only that's not what his pops wants to hear out of my mouth. I don't know what I'd do with my trophy now. I just know it's not going to mean shit to me, compared to before.

I'm a step back off my man. He scores on a jumper from deep in the corner, and I probably couldn't have stopped him anyway.

It's down to a four-point lead.

The ball's in my hands, and while the score's under the point spread, half of everything I fucked up is off my back. But I don't feel one damn bit of that weight disappear.

There's a stop in play, and two kids off our bench scramble to the scorer's table. One of them looks me in the eye and jogs straight for me.

"I'm in for you, Mustard," he says, slapping my hand.

"I told you we'd wear their starters down," yells Fat Anthony. "Just a matter of time. Get 'em off the court!"

Only I could hear in Anthony's voice how he didn't mean it. How he doesn't need for me to be sitting.

I shake my head at Mitchell, like taking me out of the game was the worst mistake he could make. But another part of me wants to rip off this Greenbacks jersey and run out of Rucker Park. Then if we win, I might not even get a trophy.

"Catch a quick blow," says Mitchell, waiting for me on the sideline. "I need you at full strength come crunch time."

Down the line, every one of our guys gives me a pound as I grab a seat at the end of the bench.

Our squad's got the ball. I don't have control over anything now. I feel the sweat stinging my eyes and my heart pounding against my chest.

A shot rattles in and out of the rim, and I jump a foot in the air.

That's when Greene slides the kid next to me out of the way and sits his ass down next to mine. I won't look him in the face for anything.

"I told Mitch I want you back on the court, pronto. I don't trust anybody with the ball but you," says Greene, chewing on the ice from a plastic cup.

I watch Stove follow the play. The whistle's always in his mouth, ready to go. He runs up and down the court, breathing hard. And no air gets into that whistle till Stove wants it to.

We score the next basket and Greene slaps me on the knee.

"Yeah!" he screams. "That's right!"

I feel his breath on the side of my face.

"Mitch, now!" yells Greene, pointing to me.

But Mitchell won't turn away from the game and puts a hand up to wave Greene off.

Both squads score, and I watch the clock tick down inside eleven minutes. I hear the ice cracking between Greene's teeth.

"You gotta get back in, Mustard," says Greene. "I need you to do your thing."

Greene grabs me by the wrist, and the cold from his fingers sends a chill through me. Then he yanks me off the bench.

Non-Fiction misses a shot, and Junkyard Dog snatches down the rebound. He looks up and sees we got a kid all alone at the other end of the court.

"Get it to him, Dog!" yells Greene, squeezing off the pulse in my wrist.

Dog's arm pulls back, and I watch the rock sail through the air. It's ten feet over everybody's head, and nobody can touch it. Then somewhere past half-court, it starts to glide down, like a bird on its wings. It lands right in our kid's hands. He lays it in, and we go up by eight points.

Mitchell pulls me away from Greene, talking right over him.

"It's our chance to bury this thing for good," says Mitchell, tapping me in the chest. "It all runs through *you* out there. Take it where it has to go."

"Everything you got, Mustard. No unfinished business," says Greene, shoving me towards the scorer's table.

All ten guys on the court fly past me as I walk over to the scorekeeper. There's a book in front of him where he keeps track of everything that happens. And he does it in pen. That way nobody can ever erase something later.

I get down on one knee in front of him, so I don't block his view.

"I'm goin' in on the next stop," I tell him.

He nods his head to me without taking his eyes off the court.

I can see the book upside down, and all the marks next to my name. There's an *X* for every basket I scored. But I know there should be marks against me, too, for everything I didn't do. And they'd probably fill up a whole page by themselves.

Fat Anthony's looking right at me, and as soon as my eyes touch his, he turns them back to the game.

The time ticks down to ten minutes flat.

Old Man Monty runs the clock. He's been doing that

job since before I was born, and Acorn calls him "Father Time."

I've heard Stove take down lots of coaches who were ready to blow because they thought they got cheated out of a few seconds.

"The time you pissed away in the beginning—that's the same time you're cryin' about now," Stove would tell them. "The game's finished. Go home and hug your family while that time's still in front of you."

I'm close enough to the see the gold face of the dude on top of the trophy. His eyes are smoothed over, and I can't tell for sure if they're open or closed. I can see the seams and grips on the ball he's holding over his head. I never noticed before, but the hand down by his side is closed tight in a fist.

A whistle finally blows, and I pop up to my feet. I feel the blood rushing to my head, and everything's spinning. But I push through till it all comes back steady again.

Stove's waving me onto the court. My eyes start at his face. Then they follow the stripes on his referee's shirt down to his shadow on the ground.

"Let's go, Mackey," I hear his voice. "Come on in."

Stove

I look at Mackey and think—he's almost a grown man.

I remember playing against J.R. a couple of years back, and suddenly, I couldn't get by him anymore. You wake up one morning and your son's stronger than you are. And while I was feeling bad about it, J.R. was flying high, because it was his turn to prove himself. But I got used to it and gave him the space he needed—as much as I thought he could handle. He never disappointed me once. It was almost the same for me with Mackey, and part of me felt like I had two sons.

But Mackey's turned into something different, or somebody poisoned him. My blood boils thinking about it. And if I find out Anthony brought any of his shit into my house, and had something to do with J.R., I'll tear him in fucking half.

I've been in plenty of fights on basketball courts. But all of them exploded out of something that happened on the spot. Maybe somebody threw an elbow, and I just lost it. It was never personal. Not like this. I never walked onto a court before looking to settle up.

Players should decide games—not referees. The best refs are invisible, and you can't even remember they were there. But I'm not about to fade into the background tonight. I'm going to do whatever I have to. And before it's over, somebody's going to see me.

13

FAT ANTHONY RAISES his arms, hollering in Hamilton's direction.

"I got a sub comin', ref! Hold on!" says Anthony.

Spider runs over to the scorer's table and yanks at his sweats. The snaps up and down the sides pop open, and the sweats fly off him with a *thip*.

The dude's all arms and legs—that's how he got the tag "Spider."

He runs right up to me and throws his feet down in front of mine. I know right away that Spider's going to shadow me everywhere I go. He's fresh off the bench, and all his energy's supposed to go into stopping me.

It's like Fat Anthony is making it easy for me now. All I have to do is let Spider cut me off from the ball, or throw a couple of passes away with him hanging all over me. Then he gets props for sticking to me like glue, and all I have to do is suck it up and say I couldn't shake him.

I start down court with Spider on my ass. His eyes are on my stomach, with his arms spread out wide. And every time I turn my feet, he switches his around, too, and keeps centered in front of me.

One of our kids tries to get the rock into my hands. But he can't because Spider's right there, playing the passing lane.

"Hold the Mustard's caught in Spider's web," says Acorn. "'Can you find the way out?' said the spider to the fly."

Now half of Rucker Park is cheering for Spider.

I keep a look on my face like it's nothing to me. That I haven't started to flash my speed yet, and that Spider's just a little mosquito I'm getting ready to swat. But before I can get free, Non-Fiction steals the ball and heads the other way with it.

J.R. and me were playing three-on-three at the park last summer when somebody on the other squad had to split. None of the regulars were left, so we asked some grown man standing on the sideline if he wanted in. "Sure," he said, and whipped off his jacket. That's when we saw that one of his sleeves was empty, and he only had one arm.

I traded looks with J.R. while the dude sprinted

across the court to get loose and jumped up at the rim with his arm stretched to the sky.

"I know the teams," the dude said, getting in front of me on defense.

I never felt more lost on a basketball court in my life. I didn't know what to do against him. I didn't want to blow by, like I needed to beat on a guy with one arm to show my skills. So I kept passing the ball off and never pulled the trigger on some wide-open shots I had. That whole time, the dude kept looking at me, like he was waiting for me to get serious and play for real.

We should have been winning easy. But the score was tied up.

"You gotta crank it up, Mackey," said J.R., tightening a fist in front of him. "I don't wanna lose to *these* guys."

Then the one-armed dude scored a basket on me down low that I didn't try to stop him on. After that point, he turned right to me with the ball tucked under his arm.

"Listen here, man," he said, stopping the game. "I watched you play for a while before I got on this court. I stepped to you on D 'cause I respect your game, and it was gonna be a challenge. That basket I scored, it means nothin'—'cause you goin' light. See, you don't show *me* any respect by playin' that way."

My tongue was cemented inside my mouth, and I just nodded my head. Then he stuck his arm out for me to slap his hand. I brought my arm down fast and heard the *smack* when our hands hit.

I drained the next shot with him up in my face. We won by a point, and took two more games after that.

I'm not sure how much I'm going to have to disrespect Spider to keep the score right. He's going to think it's his two good arms and legs that got me off my game. But it's not.

Non-Fiction cuts the lead to six points. Spider's up in my grill, and I jet past him to get the ball. Then I throw on the brakes, so I can get everyone set up and run the show.

Junkyard Dog's got Bones on his backside down low. It's a mismatch—Bones doesn't have anywhere near the size to keep Dog from going where he wants. But the two of them are locked up tight, going at each other for everything. Dog is pushing in with all his strength, and Bones is trying to shove him out the same.

Their expressions are exactly alike—the muscles in their faces and all across their foreheads are straining. That's how J.R. looked anytime he went after you on the court. It's what I see in his pops's face tonight, too.

Dog sticks one arm up to tell me he's ready for the

ball. I cock the pass over my head, and they brace their bodies against each other's one last time, scrapping for position.

Suddenly every muscle in Bones's body goes soft, and he backs away. Only Dog is still pushing. It's one of the oldest tricks in the yard, and something Stove used to pull on J.R. and me. Without Bones pushing back, Dog loses his balance and goes falling backwards to the floor. That's when I let go of the pass, and it sails out-of-bounds.

"Timber!" screams Acorn. "That was a mighty big tree to cut down."

The crowd is howling over Dog hitting the deck.

I stare at Stove like maybe he wants to blame me for pulling the chair out from under Dog's ass. The scorekeeper's making a mark in his book. I know he's putting a turnover next to my name for throwing that pass away.

"That should be a foul!" shouts Greene. "He made him fall!"

"Greenie, you think that's a foul?" roars Fat Anthony. "I think you been rappin' yourself in the head too long."

Mitchell's trying to calm Greene down, explaining why the play's good. But Greene doesn't want to hear it.

"That's punk-ass shit," snaps Greene as Bones jogs past.

Junkyard Dog's super-hyped now. He's got on a frigid ice-grill, and his beams are fixed on Bones. Then halfway down court, Dog's shoulder slams into Bones's. But Bones stiffens up on the hit, throwing his shoulder, too.

"Just one time I'll let that go!" Stove warns them.

There's almost eight minutes left, and it feels like the time's moving in slow motion. Kodak's got the ball for Non-Fiction, and forces a shot up with one of our kids all over him.

"No! No! N—" starts Fat Anthony, till the shot slips through the net. "Yeah, baby! Yeah!"

Kodak keeps his feet fixed to that spot for a second, with his wrist frozen in a perfect gooseneck for everybody to see.

"That's what coaches call a good/bad shot," says Acorn. "The only thing good about it was it went in."

I start back up court with the ball and hear everything break loose ahead of me. So I bend my neck around Spider to see. It's Dog and Bones. They're tangled up together, throwing blind punches past each other's heads.

"Ooooooh!"

The crowd gets louder with every miss, till Dog connects on one. Then the noise jumps to another level.

Dog pulls his fist back from Bones's temple, looking to nail him again. But Bones shoves both hands up under Dog's throat, knocking him back. The cops come rushing onto the court, and I can't tell the refs' whistles from police whistles.

Bones wrestles Dog to the ground, and Stove gets on top of them before the cops. He's got an arm over each of their necks and won't back off, no matter what the cops tell him.

"This is for the refs, not police!" screams Stove from the pile.

That's when the cops let Hamilton in, and he pulls Bones clear.

The crowd cheers as Stove walks Junkyard Dog back to the bench and hands him to Mitchell instead of the cops.

"They both threw punches," Stove tells the score-keeper. "They're both gone from the game."

"Why my guy, Ham? Why my guy?" screams Fat Anthony. "He was only defending himself!"

But Hamilton just shakes his head.

It's almost natural for those two to mix it up. Bones won't bend on anything, and Dog can't take it when somebody gets the best of him. So *bang!* It's on. But a few days from now, they'll probably be on the same side in some pickup game, fighting to win together and watching each other's back.

It's not that simple for *me*—things won't snap back like that. And I can't get even with anybody, because it's me who caused it. Maybe J.R.'s pops can get revenge, but I know that's going to touch me, too.

Stove starts over to me for the rock. I flip it to him, like that could stop him from getting any closer. Then he points to the sideline for somebody on our squad to put the ball back in play. Only I won't budge, and some other kid runs over.

There's seven and a half minutes left to play. But that's game-time. The clock gets held up on every stop in between, and nobody knows for sure how long it'll take for everything to get decided.

Fat Anthony

Some things you can't set up. They give them to you gift wrapped. Bones for Dog—that's a trade I'll take right now. They lose twice as much as we do 'cause they got to lean even more on Mustard.

Down by just four points—I can feel the momentum switching to us. I'm gonna win this bet and the championship, too. I see it comin', so let me tell Father Time on the clock to cool his heels, and let it flow natural.

Monty's been down with me forever. I never talk to him and he never talks to me. The money just shows up in his pocket come tournament time. Monty wraps the plug to the clock around his leg nice and tight. Then every time he leans back, the plug edges out of the socket and cuts the juice. I can get an extra eight or ten seconds a minute that way when we're on the wrong side of a score. But things are lookin' good now, and I'll give him the sign to back off.

That's right—look at me, Mustard.

Fuss with that damn Spider, too.

Let me fill up your mind till there's too much to think about.

14

SPIDER'S HAWKING ME all over the court. He thinks he's the shit and that he's got my number. I hate that everybody else is probably thinking that, too. He's way up in my face, and I finally shove him off to get free. That's when Stove blows his whistle and shoots an arm straight out to show everybody what I did.

"Good call, ref! Good call!" yells Fat Anthony, clapping his hands. "That Mustard must be piss-yellow now!"

Spider takes the ball out on the sideline next to Fat Anthony, with me guarding him. I can see the sweat on Anthony's neck and the flesh flapping under his chin when he opens his mouth. Then Fat Anthony lifts his eyes up to mine. He knows exactly what I am inside, and how it took just five hundred bucks for me to sell out my team.

"Better not let your daddy down," says Fat Anthony as Spider inbounds the ball.

Stove waves both arms over his head, stopping the clock.

"Don't you talk to a player on another team," says Stove, straight to Anthony's face. "I'm warning you, I won't let you disgrace this game."

"I'm talkin' to my kid! You hear me? *My kid!*" explodes Fat Anthony. "Don't get between me and my players, Stove!"

"You get a second technical, you'll be out of this game," Stove warns him. "I'll make you leave the park."

Greene's going ballistic from our bench.

"I already showed you once how I set traps for rats, Fat Man," snarls Greene. "Keep away from my boyz, 'cause next time I settle up with *you!*"

His words rip right through me. I'm shaking all over, and if I could, I'd curl up on the court, crying my eyes out like a little baby.

Stove steps back from Fat Anthony to look at me good. I know he heard everything out of Greene's mouth, and I can see his eyes turn to fire.

I wish I could jump into Stove's arms. I'd hug him tight and bury my face in his chest. I'd tell him how he's been like my second pops. That J.R. was my blood brother, and I'll never have another friend like him. But he'd probably spit in my face and tell me how he hated my guts. That I don't deserve to call anybody family.

"Let's finish this!" demands Stove, emptying his lungs into his whistle.

Non-Fiction brings the ball up court, and my mind's everywhere but on the game. Spider's cutting back and forth, and I just follow him. I'm almost numb inside, and only my legs are still strong. So I keep on running, trying to hold my balance.

Kodak nails another tough shot, and our lead's down to two points, 65 to 63.

Spider's set in front of me, and I want to slap the confidence right off his face. I throw my feet into high gear. He bites hard at every fake, and the crowd roars as I make him dance.

"Spider needs a new pair of socks," says Acorn. "He just got juked out of his."

I blow by him and miss an easy layup.

I can't look anybody in the face, so I watch the ball get passed around, and the seconds slip off the clock.

The next time Kodak touches the rock, he dribbles straight into the teeth of our defense. There's nothing in his eyes but basketball. No fear. No thinking. Nothing. And I'm jealous to my bones. Then Kodak plants a foot and pulls up. The defense slides past him, and he lets loose a one-handed floater that finds the bottom of the basket.

"Good gracious! That boy's in *the Zone!*" blasts Acorn. "This game's all even."

The Zone's a place where your mind and body are on the exact same wavelength. You make moves without thinking about them, and everything's natural and pure.

A thousand things can creep into a shooter's head and screw him up—the defense, the crowd, or anything you carry onto the court with you. You start thinking about every part of your stroke and get thrown off. But when you're in the Zone, you might as well be on the court alone, because nothing can get close to you. It's just you and the basket. There's no pressure, and everything just flows like it's supposed to.

But I know I'll never find that feeling again. Not on a basketball court. Not anywhere.

It's crunch time, and kids on our squad are looking for me to take over.

I pass the ball off to one of our guys, then he pushes it right back at me. It happens again with the next kid, and I feel like I'm playing Hot Potato.

One of our kids steps up and sets a solid screen on Spider. I pop free, with a wide-open shot staring me in the face.

"That's automatic!" somebody screams from our bench.

I raise up to shoot, but none of it comes natural. It's like there's a hundred pieces to my stroke, and I got to build one on top of the other. My eyes are zeroed in on the front of the rim. But just before I release the rock, everything I've done flashes through my mind in fast-forward. Then, before I can blink, it's gone with the shot.

The ball hits iron and goes straight up in the air. Everybody's fighting for position, and Kodak presses his body up against mine to block me off from the basket. When the ball can't go any higher, I see the seams stop spinning. It floats down, and falls through the heart of the basket, without even jiggling the net.

We're back in front by a basket, and Mitchell's chasing me down the sideline.

"Mustard! Mustard, stay on Kodak!" he yells. "Be the stopper!"

I stay in front of Kodak and try to cut him off from the ball. If he's in the Zone, I don't want him bringing that at me, because I got nothing inside me to stand up against it now.

Non-Fiction misses their next shot, and I chase down the rebound. Spider comes flying at me, and Kodak, too. They're both right on top of me, with their arms straight up. I'm trapped in the corner and can't see past. I bring the rock into my stomach to protect it. It feels like it weighs a ton, and it's all I can do to hold on. Then I feel myself falling out-of-bounds.

"Time-out!" I scream.

I hear Stove's whistle and drop the rock to the floor.

The clock's frozen solid with three minutes and three seconds to play.

Our kids are clapping for me, and Mitchell comes up the sideline to meet me.

"Heads-up play, Mustard. You saved us a possession," says Mitchell, walking me back to the bench.

"The championship and more!" says Greene, putting a fist into the chest of every kid coming off the court.

But when it's my turn, I close my eyes and try to shut out every word. Then I feel the bump from his fist, and it's like getting shoved out of a nightmare into something even worse.

Mitchell's telling everybody what he wants us to do. Only I'm still not listening to anything outside of my heart beating.

Junkyard Dog squeezes my shoulder, like everything he ever wanted was riding on *me* now. I look down, and J.R.'s initials are staring back at me from everybody's kicks. Then Mitchell breaks the huddle and looks me in the eye.

"Mustard, all the real hot dogs are sitting in the stands wishing they were playing for the championship," he says. "You're a leader. These kids look up to you 'cause you got the guts to go out there for you and J.R."

"And don't let that fat fucker get in your ear," says Greene, getting in front of my face. "I'm countin' on you to be *my* boy."

I look into Greene's shades and see my reflection—one in each eye. I don't know which one is Mackey, and which is Hold the Mustard. I don't know how they got split like that, or if they were ever both the same. I just know that I can't stand the sight of either one of them.

Stove comes back from the scorer's table holding a silver stopwatch. Then he calls Fat Anthony and Mitchell together.

"Coaches, I'm not confident in the way that clock's been moving," says Stove, showing them the face of the watch in his hand. "I'm gonna keep the time on the court, too, to check it. I just want you to understand that in the end, my time's what we're gonna live by."

I step back onto the middle of the court, but nothing's changed for me. None of the clocks have moved a second, and it's like I'm still trapped in that corner of the court.

15

I'M SHADOWING KODAK when a Non-Fiction player throws a pass away. The ball's headed out-of-bounds, and Kodak's streaking to save it. I stick right with him, and the scorer's table comes up fast.

I've been holding something back ever since that morning I took Fat Anthony's money. First I held back on J.R., thinking I could hide it from him. Now I'm holding back the truth from Stove and screwing over the team. Only I can't play that line anymore.

Kodak dives across the table for the ball, and so do I.

I don't care if I break a leg or crack my skull wide open. It's better than being backed into a corner with no way out.

The scorekeeper grabs his book off the table.

Kodak reaches the rock first, slapping it backwards. It hits square in my hands and I shove the ball back off

Kodak last. Then I go crashing through the trophy and land upside down on the ground with it cradled inside my arms. The marble bottom's jabbing me in the stomach, and the gold ball that kid holds is pressed up against my throat.

I swallow hard, and feel for every part of me. But nothing's broken.

Then I get pulled back up to my feet and hear all the arguing.

Hamilton's saying the ball was off me last. That the rock belongs to Non-Fiction. I know he's wrong, and maybe Fat Anthony finally got the call he's been working Hamilton for all game.

"Thank you, Mr. Hamilton. Thank *you*," says Fat Anthony. "That's what we need here—a sharp set of eyes."

Kodak's already back on the court. And when Stove sees I'm still in one piece, he yanks the trophy away from me, setting it back on the table right.

Mitchell and Greene are both blowing a fuse.

"Christ, Hamilton! You couldn't see that from the other side of the court!" argues Mitchell. "Stove, you were closest to it. Why didn't you make the call?"

"It's more bullshit! That's why!" shouts Greene.

Then Greene turns away from the refs. I watch his whole body start to coil. He rips his shades off and stares straight at me. His eyes are blacker than anything I've ever seen, and they drill two holes into the deepest part of me.

"What are you jumpin' over tables with that joker for? The ball was gonna be off them," hisses Greene. "What, you wanna be somebody's hero now?"

My heart's beating wild. I can't control my breathing, and if I wanted to run, I couldn't.

THAT'S HOW I felt when Greene put the knife to my throat in the park—that day we were supposed to play his squad for the first time. It got back to him that Fat Anthony had a kid on the Greenbacks in his pocket, and that the bet was in the bag.

"It's either you, or you know who it is!" demanded Greene, backing me up against the fence with his posse circled around.

The couple of kids hanging around the park all jet.

Greene started rattling off names of kids on our squad, and I was scared shitless.

J.R. and me had covered for each other hundreds of times before on anything that would ever go wrong. So when he got to J.R.'s name, I just nodded my head, thinking that would buy some time till I found a way out.

Then Greene pushed me down on a bench and was

pumping me for more when J.R. walked into Rucker Park. Greene hid the knife inside his hand, and J.R. walked over to us blind. My eyes were screaming out for him to run. But he didn't see it in my face till he was right on top of us.

"I hear your moms went and died 'cause she was too ashamed to look at a piece of shit like you," snapped Greene, stepping onto the court with J.R.

J.R. looked over at me quick, but I was empty inside.

"I thought that's how you got sent to that group home!" J.R. shot back.

Greene turned to his posse, slapping his knee and pretending to laugh. Then he flashed them the knife, and rammed it into J.R.'s stomach.

I just sat there frozen with every muscle tied up so tight I couldn't move.

J.R. was doubled over on the court, screaming in pain.

"You did-n't see a fuck-in' thing!" Greene told me, stabbing the air with every syllable.

Then him and his posse took off running and bounced into their rides.

"Mac-key!" J.R. cried one time, reaching his hand out to nothing.

Then J.R.'s eyes closed for good, and I bolted, too, because it was like I murdered him myself.

■ ■ ■

"THAT WAS A pure hustle play, divin' for the ball like that," says Mitchell, getting in front of Greene. "That's the kind of effort we need. You just gotta use your head more, Mustard."

My mouth's bone dry as Stove puts the ball back in play.

Kodak gets hold of the rock, and everybody else wearing a white jersey clears away. It's an isolation play, and he's supposed to take me one-on-one.

We're just a few feet from where J.R. got killed.

I set myself in front of him, bending at the knees. I lift my heels off the floor. I'm up on my toes, and all my weight's balanced on the balls of my feet.

Kodak juts his jaw to the left, and every part of me jumps that way. I should be watching his stomach, but I can't take my eyes off his face. That's what I want to see again when I look in the mirror—a baller on fire, not some rag doll with its stuffing knocked out.

I bite at another bluff, and my body nearly bends in two. Then I jerk my feet back underneath me and chase after Kodak as he blows by. I have to catch him, because there's nothing left for me if I don't.

Kodak sprints for the hoop, raising the ball in one hand for the layup. I feel something run up through me from the ground, then an explosion in my legs. I leap forward with every bit of strength I can find. Then I reach across Kodak's body, and slap the rock out of his hand.

I hear the crowd in my ears and Acorn blasting something over the mike. But none of that matters to me anymore.

Stove blows his whistle, pointing at me for the foul.

I turn to the scorekeeper, lifting one hand up high to show I'm guilty.

Kodak's headed to the foul line with a chance to tie the game. I keep watching his face. He thinks I'm staring him down, trying to put a chill into him, so he steps to me.

"Peace to your partner who fell on this court," says Kodak, kissing two fingers and touching them to his heart. "But *you* were never the player people made you out to be. And you can kiss my ass every time I go by you."

"Word to yours and mine—I don't care what I have to do, I'm keepin' in front of you," I answer.

Kodak buries the first foul shot, without ever taking his eyes off the rim. He doesn't move his body out of place an inch, ignoring his players along the foul line who want to slap his hand. Then I watch his release again. It's identical to the first. Only this time the rock doesn't go down, and rattles out of the rim.

"Shit!" screams Kodak as our squad grabs the rebound with a one-point lead.

Non-Fiction's pressing us, and Fat Anthony's pushing them. I got control of the rock with the clock running down, and the silver watch in Stove's hand. But I'm in no hurry.

"No laying back!" screams Greene. "Bring it, Mustard! Bring it!"

When the time slips inside of two minutes, the crowd gets on its feet and starts to really make noise. I know Greene and Fat Anthony are sweating out every second, and all they can do now is wait on me to move.

Spider gets up too close, and I rocket past. I sidestep two more defenders and let loose a little teardrop shot. The rock rims out, but I hold my ground and rip down the rebound. I throw my head up in the air, and another dude goes flying for the fake. I lay the ball up, but Kodak comes out of nowhere and gets a piece of it.

"It just won't go down!" says Acorn.

The rock's three feet over my head, with Kodak fighting me for it all the way.

That's when I feel two giant springs uncoil in my legs. I rise up over Kodak and tap the ball into the basket with one hand.

"Hold the Mustard 'cause you won't need any. That boy's already spiced up with desire!" echoes Acorn. "Greenbacks lead by three points."

Fat Anthony calls time-out, ripping into his team.

"Kick his fuckin' ass out there before I kick every one of yours!" yells Anthony, without stopping for a breath. "The game's on the line, and you're gonna let that piss-ass little nothing turn big!"

But nobody on their squad *let* me—I stepped up, and there's no turning back.

Everybody on my side's slapping my hand. Stove's telling both coaches there are no time-outs left, and now nobody can stop the clock from moving.

I move closer to our bench, but I won't step off the court. I want my feet planted where J.R. and me started something together. The other kids stick close to me, and Mitchell moves the huddle out to where I'm standing.

I look Greene in the eye, like there was never a second I was scared of him, and that he's going to pay for killing J.R.

He tries to turn up the heat by glaring back, but it's too late.

Whatever's inside of me is already on fire.

So Greene puts his shades back on and starts jawing at the team.

"You all know what's ridin' on this game for me," says Greene. "Do *not* fuck this up!"

I hear the words slither off Greene's tongue, and my eyes get fixed on that kid on top of the trophy.

16

I LOOK DOWN and push my toes up against the line. I see J.R.'s initials on my kicks, and I can feel him standing with me. My body's straight, and both arms are high over my head. The crowd's pressed up at Kodak's back. Stove's about to hand him the ball, and I'm already jumping up and down, trying to block Kodak's view.

"Mustard's not givin' him enough room," says Fat Anthony. "My guy's supposed to get two feet clear."

That's when Stove reaches out and puts his hand against my chest. His shoulder moves, but he doesn't push me back an inch.

"We gotta do the right thing here, Mackey," says Stove, starting his count.

Non-Fiction inbounds. They keep setting screens to bump me off Kodak, till they finally get him the ball. The clock's running down, and I know Kodak can't waste time faking. He looks left, so I figure he's going right, and I got the sideline there to help me out. Kodak explodes out of his shoes, and I slide right as far as I can. But he jets past through the open space between my foot and the line, flying to the rim.

I hear Stove's whistle as Kodak scores, and think maybe somebody fouled him going to the hoop. Only Stove's down on one knee, slamming the sideline with an open hand to show where Kodak stepped out-of-bounds.

The basket doesn't count.

"His foot never touched the line!" screams Fat Anthony, nearly jumping out of his skin. "What are you tryin' to pull here, Stove? Are you in on this, too, Ham? Are you part of this?"

Stove brings the rock to the sideline, and I run over to put it in play. Fat Anthony comes up behind Stove, screaming at him. But Stove won't turn around and follows the play up court.

There's less than a minute left, and we're ahead by three points. We don't have to shoot the ball—all we need to do is hold on to it tight, and kill off the clock. But Greene's got our kids juiced over the spread, wanting us to score big for him. So somebody hoists up a crazy shot from the corner that misses by a mile. But Non-Fiction can't haul in the rebound, and the ball's rolling loose underneath our basket. I'm the first one to hit the floor for it. Only I can't control it, and now I'm at the bottom of the pile, looking up through arms and legs.

Fat Anthony's squad finally grabs the ball. I get the last guy off of me, and I'm almost to my feet when Kodak shoves me back down and bolts the other way.

I feel the skin scrape off my knee, and the sting when the air first hits it.

Without me, Non-Fiction's got numbers, playing us five-on-four.

"We need you back, Mustard!" calls Mitchell, waving me up court.

That's when Spider gets stripped of the rock, and one of our kids rifles it up ahead to me. I'm all alone. There's nobody within forty feet of me, and there's nothing to think about.

I take a few easy dribbles with the crowd screaming off the hook.

"Better hold your breath!" announces Acorn, like I'm about to tear the rim in two.

I go to plant my foot, and I feel my ankle twist. I'm going to fall flat on my face, and a giant *gasp* rushes into my ears. But I take the weight off my ankle fast, before it turns over, and pull up every bit of strength I ever got from growing up on this court with J.R. And right then,

I believe in myself more than anything—that there's no way I'm going down. My stomach muscles turn to steel, and I straighten myself back up.

I take one last dribble and lay the rock home.

"Hold your breath for sure," says Acorn. "It's a five-point lead, and thirty-two seconds to go by the big clock."

I can hear Greene and Fat Anthony yelling over everybody, with their voices hitting head-on. Non-Fiction's playing frantic. They miss their next shot, and I drop my body on Kodak's, so he's got no prayer of grabbing a rebound.

Our kid puts the ball into my hands, but I don't want it. I don't want any part of settling this damn bet, so I pass it off quick.

Both squads come up empty, shooting blanks. Non-Fiction misses their last shot, and the ball ricochets off the iron, right to me. I zigzag past kids with it, so nobody can touch me. And when the clock hits one second, I throw the ball high up to the stars for J.R. to share the championship. But Kodak jumps in front of me, and I bounce off his chest to the ground.

"That's for you, Hot Dog," sneers Kodak.

The crowd starts to come onto the court, but Stove's blowing his whistle, so the cops push everybody back.

"There's one second left by my watch," Stove shouts to the scorekeeper. "Mackey to the line. That was a two-shot foul."

"Yeah! Yeah! That's what I'm talkin' 'bout!" hollers Greene, surrounded by his posse. "Those are *my* Greenbacks! Better start countin' it out, Fat Man!"

But Fat Anthony's busy hustling his squad off the court, like the game's over.

"We're not finished here," says Stove, running over to Anthony. "You don't put your players back on this court, I'll just give the Greenbacks two points. And I promise you—you'll never have another team in this tournament."

Fat Anthony never opens his mouth and pushes five of his guys onto the court.

The crowd's pressed up along the sidelines, waiting to bust loose, and the cops start a human chain to hold them back.

Every kid in a green jersey is celebrating, and everybody wearing white looks like they just had their heart torn out and shoved back under their nose.

I set my feet at the foul line, and Stove walks the rock out to me. His face is calm as can be. Only his eyes are raging, and we both know there's more to this than two lousy foul shots.

"Congratulations, Mackey," says Stove in an even

voice. "This is where you always wanted to be—with everything ridin' on you. Now—*juega con fuego*. Show me what you're really made of."

I look over at the scorer's table, and Greene's got the gold trophy in his filthy hands. Then Greene shakes it at me, tilting it sideways, till that kid on top isn't reaching up to the sky anymore. He's just reaching out to nothing.

"Make it sweeter for me, Mustard," says Greene. "Make it even sweeter."

I take a few dribbles to get my rhythm. Then I run my hands across the seams, feeling for the grips. And I can't remember when a rock ever felt heavier in my hands.

Fat Anthony's eyes are nailed into my side. But he's not grilling me like I better miss these two free throws. He's looking at me like I fucked him every step of the way tonight. That I was a traitor to both sides.

I let the air out of my lungs, then I bow my head. I raise up with the shot, and the ball slams off the backboard, two feet off to the side of the rim.

"Brick!" screams somebody in the crowd, but Acorn doesn't say anything.

I step back off the line and look over my shoulder. Greene's up at the edge of the court, and I stare into his shades. If I was close enough, I'd slap them off his face just to see if his eyes could turn any blacker.

"I see it's about you and me, Mustard," says Greene. "Don't worry, one-on-one's my style, too. Make the damn shot!"

Stove delivers the ball to me on one bounce, and it sticks in my hands. I close my eyes to shut everything else out. When I open them again, it's just me and the rim, and I might as well be shooting baskets by myself in the morning.

Inside my mind, I can see my stroke and feel the rock rolling off my fingertips like a feather. I can see J.R. standing inside his good kicks, watching me. My whole life, I wished I could be as strong as him.

That's when I raise up and fire the rock over the backboard. I watch it sail through the dark sky, till it lands deep in the crowd. Then the cool air slips back into my chest. And it's like losing a weight from around my neck that had dragged me so far down I didn't remember how to stand up straight anymore.

I hear Anthony laughing his fat ass off, but I don't give a shit about him. My eyes are glued to Greene as he steps onto the court, stabbing the air with his finger.

"Yeah! You were the fuckin' rat!" explodes Greene.

"Murderer! You killed J.R.!" I scream at the top of my lungs.

Greene slams the trophy down, and it bounces two feet off the ground. Then he comes charging after me.

His footsteps pick up speed, and my heart pounds faster. I drive my legs into the ground, waiting on him. Then for a second, I lose sight of him, like I blinked too long.

But it was Stove who cut in front of me.

He hooks his arm under Greene's neck, stopping him cold in his tracks. Then Stove jerks Greene backwards, slamming him to the ground. His hands are wrapped around Greene's throat, pounding the back of his head on the concrete, over and over.

"What did you do?" screams Stove, with every *crack* of Greene's skull. *"What did you do?"*

My legs never move. I stay planted in that one spot, like I was a tree with roots running deep into Rucker Park.

The cops surround the two of them, and let Stove get in a few more good licks before they wrestle him off Greene. It takes three strong cops to pull Stove away. But he won't quit trying to get back at that fuck. And every time Stove spins those cops around, his eyes catch sight of mine.

I know the time's coming soon when I'm going to have to stand up in front of him and take whatever Stove's got for me.

Greene's laid out on the court, moaning with his eyes half shut. There's a pool of blood under his head, and two EMTs are just starting to work on him. I look around for his posse, but they've all bounced.

I lift my feet from the floor and go to pick up the trophy. I'd rather find it smashed to pieces than see Greene holding it.

The ball's broke off from that kid's hand, and the gold plating's chipped off his shoulder. He's nothing but plastic underneath. But I guess I always knew that.

Hamilton calls the game a final—Greenbacks 71, Non-Fiction 66.

Then the scorekeeper signs his name at the bottom of the book, closing it shut.

Epilogue

NOW THAT SCHOOL'S started up again, I mostly play ball there—in the gym at George Washington High School. I only come here to Rucker Park on weekends, early in the morning when it's empty.

I bow my head at the spot where J.R. got killed. Then I start shooting around, trying to find my rhythm. Sometimes when the ball's going down and everything's flowing good, I forget about what happened for a while, and it's almost like I'm forgiven.

Only this Sunday it's different. Stove just walked into the park.

He leans up against the fence watching me, and my hands are trembling so bad I can hardly keep a grip on the ball.

The morning after the championship game, I was

sitting on the steps outside our building when Stove finally got home. He was still wearing his referee's shirt from the night before. I'd told the cops at the station house everything, and I knew by the cold look on Stove's face that he'd already heard it all from them.

My mouth started to make the words "I'm sor—"

Till Stove snapped right through that.

"I don't wanna hear it from you. Not one miserable excuse. And after all I told you 'bout getting mixed up with Anthony," he said, raising a finger to the sky. "God as my witness—I never want to hear it said out loud again."

But the story got said out loud a lot, on TV and the radio. It was on the front page of the *Daily News*, too— *BASKETBALL BET BRINGS BETRAYAL AND MURDER.*

I couldn't even explain what I'd done to my own mother without her looking at me like she'd raised some kind of street punk who didn't care about anybody but himself. And her damn husband wouldn't even talk to me after that.

Greene got charged with J.R.'s murder.

The cops arrested him while he was in the hospital with a concussion, and cuffed him to the bed. Then Greene bought the biggest lawyer he could, who's making it sound like J.R. put the knife in Greene's hand himself, and then ran into it. Greene's even got a new rap out about how he's being framed, called "Rucker Park Setup."

I'd run into Stove every couple of days—either on the stairs in our building, or while he was delivering the mail. It was always tense, and I can't come close to looking him in the eye.

College coaches who haven't heard about what happened still write me with scholarship offers. I know every one of those letters passes through Stove's hands. And maybe he still gets some for J.R., too.

Since the tournament finished, Fat Anthony's been almost invisible. I thought he might come around looking for his five hundred dollars back. But he probably got his money's worth watching Stove kick the shit out of Greene.

I didn't ever want to touch that money again. So I dropped the balled-up pair of sweat socks where I'd kept it into the Salvation Army box, just to get another step clear.

I saw J.R.'s picture through the window of Acorn's barbershop. It's hanging over the big mirror, right up front. But I wouldn't go inside and take what dudes there would dish out for anything.

"There's *Mackey*," said Acorn to me the one time I saw him on the street.

His voice punched my name hard, like I wasn't good enough to be blessed with one of his tags anymore, and be called "Hold the Mustard."

Mitchell pulled up in front of my building one night, popping open his trunk.

"I don't think you deserve shit. But the team voted five to four to give you one of these," he said, pushing a trophy at me. "I usually wouldn't waste my time on somebody that played his best friend and team like *you* did. But I never got suckered into coaching for a scumbag like Greene before neither."

I felt ashamed to be holding it, with that perfect gold kid on top. So I pointed to the broken trophy in Mitchell's trunk—the one that Greene slammed to the ground that night.

"If it's all the same, Coach, I'd rather take that one," I said, and traded for it.

Mitchell started up the stairs with J.R.'s trophy to give to Stove. I stayed on the first floor, listening to his footsteps climb every flight. Then I heard Mitchell knock on the door and the locks turn open.

Later, Stove pulled up the shade and put the trophy in J.R.'s bedroom window for everybody in the neighborhood to see. I didn't know where to keep my trophy, so I stood it up in the hallway next to J.R.'s good kicks.

And after a few days, I got it into my head that it was already in the right place.

But nothing feels right out here now—not with Stove grilling me like that.

Then Stove crosses onto the court and starts feeding me the ball. The shots leave my fingertips for the rim, but not a single one connects.

"I still don't know if I hate you or what," says Stove, nearly knocking me over with a pass. "It changes back and forth all the time."

That's when I pull up all courage I can find and, with my voice shaking, I answer, "I don't blame you one bit. I can't figure it out about myself, either."

Basketball season never ends. It's just the calendar that runs out of pages. When the weather turns cold, the run across the city moves from schoolyards to gyms. If you can't find a roof to play under, you cut the fingers out of an old pair of gloves and let the sweat pour off your head under a wool cap, till the hair that curls out from the back gets covered in icicles. The ball gets smooth like glass, and the frozen air inside keeps it from bouncing back up off the concrete.

Like the kids say, "That's old school."

That means it's got heart, and has earned your respect.

The run in the street opens up again when the wind can't blow a jump shot off line anymore. Kids who nobody picked for their sides last time around have shot up like bean stalks. The NCAA tournament is all over the tube, and they call it "March Madness." That's when everybody falls in love with the game again.

Soon, school lets out for summer, and it's like a paradise. The courts are packed with players every day, till the sun goes down. Then some players move to the court closest to the streetlamp, or turn up the headlights on a car to see.

Growing up, I'd listen to the balls bouncing outside my window at night, like a lullaby. Sometimes I still do.

Rucker Park Setup

When the dog days roll around, you can fry an egg on the asphalt at half-court. So you take your sneakers off and run through the sprinklers to keep cool. That's when they hold the big tournament at Rucker Park, and it's like a block party for basketball junkies. The tournament's more important to kids along Eighth Avenue than the NBA finals, because it's all about their neighborhood. Players from all over the city come to prove themselves here.

I've spent almost fifty years feeling my soul take root on this patch of ground. But I only mention the time for anyone who lives by the calendar. Like I said, there's no off-season in basketball. The run in New York City never dries up, and won't even get buried with the next Ice Age.

That why dinosaurs like me will never go extinct.